★ Americ

Like Sisters

Zoe Is on the Air

By Clare Hutton

Scholastic Inc.

Published by Scholastic Inc., *Publishers since 1920.* SCHOLASTIC and associated logos are trademarks and/or registered trademarks of Scholastic Inc. The publisher does not have any control over and does not assume any responsibility for author or third-party websites or their content.

Book design by Maeve Norton
Illustrations by Helen Huang

ISBN 978-1-338-11504-8

10 9 8 7 6 5 4 3 2 1   18 19 20 21 22

Printed in the U.S.A.   23
First printing 2018

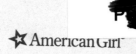
Like Sisters

Zoe Is on the Air

Chapter One

"I am *so* glad it's finally almost spring!" Zoe Martinez said, dropping her backpack on the floor of the history classroom and flopping into her seat. "I couldn't take another *week* of winter."

"Aw, come on," her twin sister, Natalia, said from across their shared table. "Who doesn't love winter? Christmas! Snow! Hot cocoa!"

"You're kind of weirdly excited about winter." Caitlin, Natalia's best friend, lined up her pencils and notebook neatly, then tucked her long curls behind her ears, smirking over at Zoe.

Zoe lived in Waverly, a small town on Maryland's Chesapeake Bay. Usually, walking around the pretty town lightened her spirits: the wide blue sky reflected in the blue of the bay, white gulls wheeling overhead, and white-sailed boats skimming across the water. Zoe loved to draw and paint, and the deep green shades of the marshy wetlands near the bay or the creamy white flowers of the magnolia trees on her family's front lawn always filled her with inspiration.

Winter was her least favorite season for Waverly, though: everything in shades of gray and brown, from the gray sky and choppy waters of the bay to the dim browns of the winter-dead grasses and trees.

Emma walked up and plopped down a stack of library books on the table before taking a seat next to Zoe. "Have you guys thought about what you want to do for our ancient civilizations project? I've been thinking about ancient Egypt, and I found these—"

Natalia bounced in her seat. "I *love* ancient Egypt. It's all, like, giant pyramids and cats and fancy gold jewelry. And mummies!" Natalia's hands flew in the air as she talked. She laughed loudly and frequently, and her long, dark hair tumbled messily around her shoulders.

Across from Natalia, Emma was listening intently, her forehead creased with concentration. Zoe knew that it was important to Emma to do things right and to get along with everyone. Emma was Zoe and Natalia's cousin, but she was like a sister to them both. She had moved to Waverly just before the start of sixth grade, and Zoe knew her cousin was still finding her place.

Caitlin flipped one of Emma's books open with a long, manicured finger. Zoe could tell from the way Caitlin's nails tapped on her desk that she was just waiting to break in with her own opinion. If Emma liked to be sure she was doing the right thing, Caitlin just liked to be *right*. Natalia and Caitlin had been best friends for ages, but until this year, that was all Caitlin had been to Zoe: her sister's best friend. But when they'd starred in *The Wizard of Oz* together—Zoe as Dorothy, Caitlin as Glinda—back in the fall, Zoe had gotten to know Caitlin better. Caitlin had helped the younger kids in the chorus with their songs, and she'd been a lot of fun to hang out with between scenes. It was true that Caitlin always thought she knew the answer to everything, but the thing was, Zoe found that Caitlin was often right.

At this moment, Caitlin's eyes shone not just with impatience but with amusement and affection, too, as she listened to Natalia rambling on about mummies:

"And then they pulled their brains out through their noses! Disgusting!"

Zoe brushed back her smooth bob and adjusted her neatly ironed top. Sometimes she felt as if she was on the outside of whatever was going on, observing everyone else instead of participating. Almost as if she was waiting for something to begin.

She rested her chin on one hand as she remembered playing Dorothy. When she'd been onstage, she hadn't felt that way, as if she was waiting for real life. She'd painted sets for drama club productions before, but when she'd played Dorothy, for the first time she'd been in the spotlight instead of watching from offstage. To her own surprise, she'd found that she liked being the focus of attention. The audience had been clapping for *her*. It made Zoe feel as happy and fizzy as if she were filling up with bubbles. *I wish I could do something that exciting again*, she thought wistfully. Maybe there would be a spring play she could try out for—

Bing. An alert sounded over the intercom, interrupting the Egypt conversation. Mr. Thomas, their history and English teacher, turned on the interactive

4

whiteboard at the front of the room. "Pay attention to the announcements, people," he called.

Yawning, Zoe looked up. Charlotte Avery and Oliver Marks, two eighth graders, appeared on screen.

"Happy Wednesday, Waverly Oysters!" Charlotte shouted, grinning widely.

Zoe rolled her eyes. *Honestly.* Sure, oysters were important to the environment and everything, as Zoe had learned in science units on the Chesapeake: They filtered and cleaned the water. They helped preserve the ecosystem. Oyster stew was tasty. Oysters no doubt had many other admirable qualities. But with all the creatures in and around the bay, why had the school chosen *oysters* as their mascot? There were otters and bottlenose dolphins in the bay! There were ospreys! Even being the Waverly Blue Crabs would have been better, if they wanted a shellfish as a mascot for some reason.

The two eighth graders began going through the morning announcements. A canned food drive, after-school tutoring, a contest to design a school T-shirt. "Finally, next week is going to be the last week of our

February show, *Max and Noah's Sports Talk*," Charlotte said. "We're looking for ideas for March's show!"

Zoe perked up. Every month a different short show aired on Wednesday mornings after the announcements. There had been a talent show program back in the fall, where different people sang or did magic tricks. And, later, a fashion show, where kids modeled sneakers one week and earrings another. Then one about pets.

Oliver leaned in toward the camera. "If you think you'd like to participate, just write up a proposal for your weekly ten-minute show—who's involved and what the main idea is—along with a short video of yourself in action. Submit your proposal and video to your homeroom teacher on Monday. The student council will pick the best show, and it'll appear right here every Wednesday morning in March."

"And, don't forget, we're looking for people to work behind the scenes, too," Charlotte added, smiling. "So, if you don't want to be in front of the cameras, maybe *working* the camera or taking care of the sound is right for you."

"And now, the final episode of *Max and Noah's Sports Talk*," Oliver said. He and Charlotte stood up and shuffled out from behind the table, and two seventh-grade boys took their places and began to talk about an upcoming NBA game. Zoe stopped listening. Basketball was *not* her thing.

A school TV show? Interest prickled inside her. She had to admit she was tempted by the prospect of taking center stage again. But what could she do for a TV show? She couldn't just sing songs from *The Wizard of Oz* all month. Zoe thought about the YouTube channels she liked. There was a video-game show that was pretty fun. She tried to imagine doing a show like that.

"Today I'm going to play the newest, hottest game around. I've gotten so many requests for this!" Zoe said to the camera as she picked up a controller. *"I'm fired up and we're going to see if I can beat the first three levels in this game . . ."*

Zoe frowned. She liked video games okay and she liked watching people play them on YouTube—if they said funny things while they were playing—but she didn't like them *that* much. And she wasn't actually good enough at video games for people to want to watch her play. And she doubted her school would want to promote video-game playing, anyway.

"Earth to Zoe!" Natalia said. Zoe blinked and realized that Natalia, Emma, and Caitlin were all staring at her. The sports show had finished and Mr. Thomas had turned off the whiteboard. At each table, groups were quietly (or not so quietly) discussing their projects.

"Sorry," she said. "I was just thinking."

"You were a million miles away," Emma told her.

Caitlin folded her arms. "We were trying to decide what we should do for our group project on ancient civilizations," she said, sounding faintly irritated. "Are you okay with ancient Egypt? I thought maybe we could do something about women in that civilization. They had a lot more rights than people realize. There were even woman pharaohs."

"Sure," Zoe said. She pictured what she knew about ancient Egypt. Hieroglyphics. Mummies. The Nile River Delta, which they'd talked about in class. Pyramids. Tomb paintings. Her fingers itched to pick up a brush and try to paint one. "Maybe we could do a model of, like, a female ruler's tomb."

"Maybe," said Caitlin, tapping her pen against her lips. "Cleopatra?"

Emma flipped open one of her books and began to page through it. "Hatshepsut was pharaoh way before Cleopatra, and was even more interesting. It says here that she ruled for a long time, and she used to dress up as a male pharaoh with the ceremonial beard and everything. Everyone knew she was a woman, but tradition was super-important to the ancient Egyptians, so she had to look like the pharaohs who came before her."

As the other girls leaned in to look at a picture of a statue in Emma's book, Zoe let her mind wander again. What were other good themes for shows? There was a cooking YouTube show she liked, but she wouldn't have access to a stove for the school show, and a ten-minute show was too short to cook anything, anyway.

There was a comedy show she liked, where two guys did dares and challenges suggested by their fans. It was funny, but . . . Zoe wrinkled her nose in disgust, thinking of a recent episode. *There's no way I'm eating a spider*, she thought. *Not even if it's already dead.*

A partner on the show might be a good idea, though,

she realized. If she had someone else with her, she wouldn't have to do all the talking herself. But who? She looked across the table at Natalia. A twin-hosted talk show? Some people were fascinated by identical twins—even identical twins who dressed and acted as differently as she and Natalia did—and that might be a hook for the show. And maybe the whole show could be about twins? Although she wasn't sure how they would stretch that topic out for a month.

Natalia struck the pose of an ancient Egyptian, hands stiff, head turned to one side, and the others laughed. Zoe shook off the idea of doing a show together. She loved her sister—and she even *liked* her sister—but loud, exuberant Natalia would take over a show without even meaning to, and Zoe didn't want people at school to only think of Zoe as her sister's quiet twin.

"Zoe!" Caitlin snapped again, sounding exasperated.

"What?" Zoe asked.

"You're still not paying attention. Do you want to work on the project at Emma's this weekend or not?"

"Oh, um, sure." There would be plenty of room to spread out art supplies at Seaview House, the Victorian mansion where Emma and her parents lived, and no little brothers to mess things up, the way there were at her own house. "Hey," she added, trying to sound casual. "Did you hear what they said about needing a new show for March?"

"Thank goodness," Natalia said, rolling her eyes. "If I have to listen to one more basketball game recap, I'm going to lose the will to live."

"I like Max and Noah's sports show," Emma said mildly.

"Well, you would," Zoe said. Emma was on a swim team and played soccer for the school team and even watched sports on TV—by choice. "You seem so normal otherwise," Zoe told her cousin, shaking her head in mock despair. Then she flicked her hair back and straightened her shoulders. "I thought I might submit an idea for a show," she told them. She felt her cheeks get warm.

"Awesome," Emma said approvingly, and the others nodded.

Zoe grinned, feeling encouraged. "I just need to think of something *amazing.*"

Chapter Two

"Rise and shine, sweethearts!" Zoe and Natalia's mom's voice rang out from their bedroom doorway, sounding *way* too energetic and upbeat for first thing in the morning.

Zoe groaned loudly and burrowed farther under her warm blankets. She could hear Natalia getting out of bed and getting dressed, her bare feet padding across the bedroom to her closet. "Whyyyyy?" Zoe whined.

"Because we promised to help out at breakfast at Seaview House," Natalia said practically. "And I'm also supposed walk a dog one of the guests brought."

"Oh, yeah. This always seems like a much better idea when it isn't actually happening," Zoe said, sitting up slowly and sliding her legs out of the bed. Goose bumps immediately popped up on her arms, and she shivered. It would have been great to go back to bed for about three hours.

Saturday brunch at Seaview House had grown more and more popular over the last few months since the bed-and-breakfast had opened, largely thanks to their uncle Brian's amazing cooking. Uncle Brian was Emma's dad, who had been a chef in Seattle before Emma and her family had moved to Waverly to open Seaview House. People from all over town turned up to join the B and B's guests in gobbling up the mouthwatering spread he put out.

It'll be fun, Zoe reminded herself as she pulled a sock out of her drawer and stared groggily at it. *Just not the getting up part.*

Natalia wrapped an arm around her shoulders. "Come on, sleepyhead," she said encouragingly. "Just think about the special breakfast Uncle Brian's going to be making for us before the official brunch starts. He knows we have to keep our strength up for a whole morning of helping out in the dining room."

It was chilly outside, frost glittering on the grass of the lawns they passed, and Zoe huddled deeper into her coat as the girls hurried the few blocks to Seaview House. Inside the house, though, it was warm, and the air smelled deliciously like something cinnamony baking.

"Yum," Zoe said. The cold walk had woken her up and, now that she wasn't half asleep, she felt pretty good about the idea of earning some money by helping out.

"I've got an appointment with a spaniel," Natalia told her, heading for the stairs. "I'll see you in the kitchen in a little bit." Natalia had started her own dog-walking business back in the fall, walking the dogs of guests at the inn.

As her sister disappeared up the stairs toward the guest rooms, Zoe looked around the luxurious front room. It looked especially cozy this morning, with the stained glass windows throwing stripes of color across plush red-velvet furniture.

One of Zoe's own paintings, which she had given Grandma Stephenson for Christmas last year, hung on the wall over the upright piano. It was a picture of a snowy egret, stiff-legged, picking its way across the deep green marshes at the edge of the bay. It was one of the paintings she was proudest of, and she blew the bird a kiss as she passed through.

The kitchen smelled like frying sausages. At the stove, Uncle Brian was tipping a pan, a thin layer of batter spreading across its bottom. He glanced up when Zoe came in and grinned at her. "Hello, favorite niece," he said.

Zoe rolled her eyes. "You say that to both of us."

"That's because you're both my favorites," he agreed.

Emma was sitting at the counter, flipping through a newspaper. Her damp hair was pulled back into a pony-tail, and she looked much more awake than Zoe felt. The plate in front of her was empty except for a few crumbs.

"You already ate?" Zoe asked.

"I had swim team practice," Emma explained. "I've been up for hours. Dad's making me another crepe, though, because I am *starving*."

"But this one is for Zoe," Uncle Brian said cheerfully. "Come choose a filling, Zo."

Zoe walked over to Uncle Brian and peeked into the bowls lined up next to the stove. Cooked apples, strawberries, chocolate sauce, lemon with sugar, goat cheese, and little pieces of ham.

"Strawberries and chocolate, please?" she requested, and Uncle Brian eased his spatula under the thin crepe and flipped it smoothly onto a plate, then filled the crepe with the warm strawberries and added a drizzle of chocolate sauce before folding it over. Zoe's mouth watered. She added a couple sausages to her plate and sat down on a stool at the counter, across from Emma.

"What does my horoscope say today?" Zoe asked, and Emma turned a page of the newspaper.

"Taurus," she read. "Take that plunge you've been thinking about. You'll see friends and family in a new light as you embark upon an adventure! The prospects are good for new endeavors."

I could use a new adventure. Zoe thought about the morning show at school again. That would be an adventure, and a new endeavor, too. If only she could think of a good topic!

"I'll save some batter for Natalia," Uncle Brian said. "Em, grab me some more eggs, I'm going to start a frittata for the breakfast buffet." Emma hopped down from her stool and got the eggs out of the refrigerator while Uncle Brian put another crepe onto a plate for her.

"Thanks, Dad," she said, and sat down, opening her paper again as she forked up a bite of crepe. "Oh, listen to this," she said to Zoe. "This woman wrote into the advice column and she says, *Dear Marian, My best friend and I have been friends since we were kids and she's a terrific person*—they always say stuff like that, right before they start complaining—*but she's always criticizing me. My boyfriend isn't good enough for me, the job I like isn't high-paying enough, I should decorate my apartment differently. Maybe it's because she wants the best for me, but I can't stand her constantly putting me down! I've tried to talk to her about this before, but she just gets upset. What should I do?*"

"Huh." Zoe ate the last bite of her crepe as she thought. She swallowed and said, "I'm not sure her friend *is* only bossing her around because she wants what's best for her. It doesn't sound like there's anything wrong with her life, it's just not exactly the way her friend thinks it ought to be. Maybe the friend is just criticizing the letter writer to make herself feel better."

"That might be true, but maybe the friend really is just trying to help her," Emma said. "But it doesn't matter, because what the friend wants isn't the same thing as what the letter writer wants. I think she needs to talk to her again and tell her that she's happy with her life the way it is, that it makes her feel bad when her friend is super-critical, and that she needs to stop."

"If she's her *best* friend, she should listen to her and want her not to feel bad," Zoe agreed. "But the person who wrote the letter says she's tried to talk to the friend and she just gets upset."

Emma shrugged. "If the friend gets mad and hurt whenever the writer doesn't agree with her, then the friend is using that to make the writer do what she wants. You can't just use your emotions against people whenever they cross you. It's not fair. It's like emotional blackmail."

Zoe looked at Emma with interest. She could definitely think of situations where other kids she knew had done that—gotten mad or sad and thrown some kind of fit just to get their own way in a game or in a disagreement with friends. "That's a really good point," she said. "Read me another one."

"Okay." Emma looked over the advice column. "Here's another good one: *I'm supposed to be getting married in three weeks. We've been dating for two years, and it seemed like the natural next step. But now that our wedding day is approaching, I'm realizing the last thing I want to do right now is be married. There are a lot of things I wanted to do on my own—travel, maybe live in a different city, try out a different career. I love my fiancé, who's very settled right in our hometown and plans to stay there, but I'm not sure I want to spend the rest of my life with him. The invitations have gone out and everything's ready for the wedding. Is this just a case of cold feet? How do I figure out what to do?"*

Zoe snorted. "It definitely isn't just cold feet," she said. "She says the *last thing* she wants to do is be married. This is somebody who needs to get out of that wedding."

"What a total disaster," Emma said, shuddering. "I can't imagine having to tell everyone that you're not getting married, after inviting them all to the wedding. But it would be worse to go through with it and then get divorced right away, or try to live with someone when you *know* marrying them was a mistake."

"What does Dear Marian say?" Zoe asked curiously.

"Um." Emma bent over the paper. "Basically, the same thing we did." She looked up, smiling. "We're clearly naturals at this."

"Yeah," Zoe said slowly. She stared at Emma, feeling like she was seeing her in a brand-new light, just as her horoscope had predicted. Emma was sensitive to people's feelings. She gave good advice. And Emma was easy to talk to.

Excitement bubbled inside Zoe. Was this her show?

As they began to help set up the breakfast buffet, Natalia came back from walking the spaniel and helped Zoe and Emma get the buffet table arranged in the dining room. On the crisp white tablecloth, the girls laid out chafing dishes full of bacon, sausage, thick chunks of frittata, and hash browns. Plates full of homemade pastries, breads, and freshly cut fruits sat among the warming dishes. Zoe took a long sniff: Everything smelled great.

The guests were beginning to trickle in, and Zoe went from table to table, taking orders for coffee, tea, and juice.

Both of her grandmothers, Abuelita and Grandma Stephenson, were sitting with her dad and their little brothers at a round table near the middle of the room.

"I want apple juice, Zoe, hurry up," Zoe's youngest brother, five-year-old Mateo, told her.

Zoe's dad frowned at him. "Let's see some manners, Mateo," he reprimanded him.

"Sorry." Mateo sat up straighter. "Apple juice, please, Zoe."

"Sure." Zoe took the adults' orders as well and moved on to the next table, feeling efficient and grown-up. The next table was occupied by an older couple who were weekend guests.

"Two lattes coming up!" Zoe said. "Go ahead and help yourself to the buffet." As she wrote down their drinks, she saw Caitlin's family come in and take the last open table.

Caitlin; her older brother, Rob; and their mom and dad were all a little dressed up. Caitlin and her mom wore dresses and her dad and brother wore blazers. Her dad even wore a tie! Zoe liked how Caitlin's family made things like going out to brunch special.

Caitlin arched an eyebrow at Zoe when she saw her looking at them and held up a bag for her to see. "I brought gold foil for the tomb," she called.

Zoe waved back, nodding at Caitlin to let her know that she'd heard her.

Zoe brushed past Emma as she headed back into the kitchen with the list of drinks the guests wanted. Emma was talking to Mr. and Mrs. Lau from down the street as their baby, Charlie, grinned up at her from his high chair, waving his plump hands. "I think Charlie would like one of my dad's cheese scones," Emma told the Laus. "They're not too sugary and they're kind of hard, which might feel good since he's teething."

Emma's a natural at giving advice, Zoe realized. *Now I just have to convince her of that.*

"I am so full I may never be able to eat again," Caitlin said, stretching luxuriously across Emma's bed.

"Me, too," Natalia said. "A very good morning for everybody!"

"The afternoon is also going to be great," Caitlin said decisively, sitting up and reaching for her bag. "I brought the gold foil, and I found a site about Hatshepsut that had a lot of pictures."

Emma opened her laptop, and Zoe and Natalia looked over her shoulder as she pulled up the page Caitlin was talking about. The statues of Hatshepsut caught Zoe's attention. The smooth face of the pharaoh wore a calm, secretive smile. "She looks like she knows something we don't," she said.

"That's not necessarily how she really looked, though," Emma reminded her. "The Egyptian statues all had a really specific stylized look."

"Hmm." Zoe leaned forward, looking at the image of a sarcophagus covered in hieroglyphics and the blue-and-gold mummy case inside it, which wore the same calm, secretive face. Whether the face was really Hatshepsut's or not, she liked it. "I could try to copy this."

"I could help make the model," Natalia spoke up eagerly. "Like, not the painting, but I could make the sarcophagus out of cardboard or something and put together the mummy case shape. And build the tomb."

"Emma and I can do most of the work on the oral report and you guys can do most of the art and model-building," Caitlin said decisively. Zoe cocked an eyebrow at her. "Uh. If that's okay with you, Emma," she added.

"Sounds good," Emma agreed. "We have a lot of boxes downstairs if we want to make, like, a mummy room. We could work on that right now."

She started to get to her feet, and Zoe held up a hand to stop her. "Wait, you guys," she said. *If we want to do an advice show, Emma and I need to do our proposal this weekend, too.* Everyone was looking at her, and Zoe's heart beat a little faster. What if nobody else thought this was a good idea? "Remember how I said I wanted to try to do a morning show for school?"

"Do you have an idea?" Natalia asked. "Hey, maybe you could do a painting show."

"No, I want . . ." Zoe turned toward Emma and started again. "You know how we were reading the advice column in the paper this morning and coming up with answers to the questions?"

"Yeah?" Emma said cautiously.

"I thought maybe we could do *that*," Zoe said. "Have people write in with their problems and give them advice. The two of us, together."

"Oh!" Emma's cheeks turned pink. She looked both intrigued and worried. "But why would people write to *us*?"

Zoe shrugged. "Why do they write to anybody? People want to be able to ask for help with their problems without anyone knowing who they are." She looked up at Emma appealingly. "I think a lot of people have things in their life they want advice on. Don't you think it would be fun?"

"I think it's a great idea!" Natalia announced. She spun around in Emma's desk chair. "*I'd* write to you!"

Caitlin was looking at them thoughtfully. "It could work," she said. "Zoe's very straightforward about what she thinks. And Emma's got a lot of empathy for people. You'd make a good team."

Natalia clapped her hands. "We'll help you film the video audition," she said eagerly. "Okay, Caitlin?"

Caitlin nodded. "Sure. It'll be fun."

Emma bit her lip. "I don't know . . ." she said. "I've got practices and—"

"Only swim team in March," Zoe said swiftly. "Spring soccer won't have started. The shows are during school, and we can plan them during lunch or after school. It's only four shows, one per week for the month of March." She could see that Emma was wavering.

"Well, the truth is I'm not sure I want to perform in front of the whole school," Emma admitted.

"I think you'd actually be great," Caitlin said. "You've got a very trustworthy quality."

"Absolutely," Natalia agreed.

"Really?" Emma ducked her head, shyly pleased. "You guys think we'd be good?"

"You're the person I want most to do this with," Zoe

pleaded. "You understand people and empathize with their problems, so you give amazing advice. Please?"

Emma hesitated. "I don't know," she said slowly. "Maybe."

"What if we just do the audition video and see how it goes?" Zoe suggested. Emma was shy, but Zoe was sure that, once she got in front of the camera, she'd realize how much fun this could be.

Emma still looked hesitant, but she smiled a tiny bit. "Okay," she agreed. "Why not?"

Chapter Three

"I'm not sure why you wanted to do this at *school*," Natalia said, rolling her eyes. "Don't we spend enough time here during the week?"

"The school entrance makes a nice background," Zoe told her, looking up approvingly at the tall brick building. "Besides, you love school."

"I like school okay on *weekdays*," Natalia grumbled. "Being here on a Sunday is just unnatural."

"Enough chatter, guys," Caitlin said playfully, handing Zoe a wireless microphone. "Let's get recording."

"Okay," Zoe said, tentatively taking the microphone. She glanced over at Emma, who was sitting on the school steps, twisting her fingers together. She looked pale and worried. "Hang on."

She went over and sat next to Emma. "Are you ready?" she asked.

"I don't know," Emma said. "I feel weird about, like, *performing* in front of people."

"Well, you swim and play soccer in front of people," Zoe reminded her. "You're not scared then."

Emma scrunched up her nose. "That's different. I'm not thinking about the people watching then."

"Don't think about them now," Zoe said encouragingly. "It's just us." She gestured to Caitlin and Natalia, who were fiddling with the video settings on Caitlin's cell phone.

"Okay," said Emma slowly. She didn't sound convinced.

Zoe felt a guilty pang. Was she pushing Emma into this? She took a deep breath. "Listen, Emma," she made herself say. "I'd love for us to do this together. And I think we'd be great. But you don't have to if you don't want to. I will completely understand."

"No, that's not it." Emma swallowed, looking down into her lap. "I *do* want to. I really do. I'm just scared."

Zoe took her cousin's cold hand. "You can totally do this," she said. "You're brave and tough, and you can give advice just as bravely as you dive into a pool in front of a whole gym of people. Game face, right?"

Taking a deep breath, Emma squeezed Zoe's hand, then let it go, a tiny smile creeping over her face. "Right. I can do this. Game face," she repeated, and got to her feet.

"High five," Zoe said, and they slapped hands, then turned to face Caitlin's camera.

"It's because of the Nile that ancient Egypt was able to become so advanced," Mr. Thomas said during history class on Tuesday, using his laser pointer to illuminate the fertile banks of the Upper Nile River. He started talking about floods and crops and irrigation, while Zoe doodled an Egyptian eye on her notebook. The Hatshepsut project was going pretty well, she thought. She really liked the stylized, stiff way ancient Egyptian art looked, elegant and formal. Her fingers itched to pick up a brush and try it.

"Hey, did you hear back about your show yet?" her friend Louise whispered from the next table.

Zoe blinked. "No," she whispered back. "I turned in the proposal yesterday to the student council, but I haven't heard anything. I think they were supposed to meet to decide right after school."

Another friend, Ava, leaned forward from her seat beside Louise. "I'm going to volunteer to work on the crew of the new show. It would be awesome if it was yours."

"Girls. Eyes up here," Mr. Thomas said warningly, and Zoe turned her attention back to the front of the room without replying to Ava. She tried to listen to the discussion on ancient agriculture—they had irrigation, apparently, in Egypt—but her mind kept turning back to the show. What if the student council rejected her proposal? An advice show was such a good idea!

The bell rang, and there was a flurry of movement as everyone gathered up their books and backpacks to head to lunch. Zoe fell into step next to her sister as they left the classroom. Lowering her voice, she said quietly, "You'll tell me if you hear someone else got the show, right? I don't want to go around talking about it if it's not going to happen." Natalia always heard all the gossip. If someone else got the show, she would probably know before Zoe did.

"Of course," Natalia said. "But you can always try again next time if you guys don't get picked this month."

"Yeah," Zoe said glumly, knowing she'd feel too discouraged to try again if they got turned down the first time.

The hall was crowded and noisy with locker doors banging and a hundred conversations echoing around them. Zoe followed Natalia toward the cafeteria. Her sister had just pushed her way through the swinging cafeteria doors when a hand touched Zoe's arm.

"You're Zoe, right?" a cheerful voice asked. Zoe turned and saw Charlotte Avery, the eighth-grade student council president, who, along with her vice president, Oliver Marks, did the morning announcements. Zoe didn't think she had ever spoken to Charlotte before—sixth graders and eighth graders didn't mix much—but she knew who Charlotte Avery was. In addition to leading student council, she was also the editor of the yearbook. She was super-friendly and seemed to bounce easily among the athletes and the bookworms and the popular kids. *Everybody* knew Charlotte, and as far as Zoe could tell, everybody liked her.

"Right. Hi," Zoe answered, her heart starting to beat a little harder. Had the student council made their decision about the show? Charlotte was smiling, but then Charlotte was usually smiling. It didn't necessarily mean that she had good news for Zoe.

"I'm so glad I ran into you!" Charlotte said, tugging on Zoe's sleeve to pull her to the side of the hall, out of the way. "We were sending a note to you through your homeroom teacher, but this is nicer."

"Yeah?" Zoe's mouth was dry.

"We picked your show!" Charlotte cheered. "Your and Emma's advice show is going to be our March program!"

"It is? Really?" Zoe said. She couldn't stop smiling. "Wow. Thank you!"

"Thank *you*!" Charlotte said. "An advice show is such a good idea." Her tone suddenly shifting from celebratory to businesslike, she added, "We do the morning announcements from the student council office. You and Emma need to be there at seven forty-five on the dot next Wednesday morning, totally prepared to do your show. If you're not prepared or not on time, we'll replace your show with another one. We had a couple good runners-up."

Zoe nodded. "Okay, no problem."

"Great!" Charlotte brightened again, her smile returning. "You'll tell Emma?"

"Of course I will!" Zoe hurried on to the cafeteria, excitement bubbling inside her.

Emma was sitting beside Natalia, dividing the special lunch Uncle Brian had packed for the three of them. Caitlin sat across from them, other friends crowding both sides of the table.

"Where'd you go?" Natalia asked as Zoe slipped into a seat across from her. "I thought you were right behind me. Anyway, look—" she went on, not stopping for an answer. "Uncle Brian made us those Vietnamese sandwiches with the pickled vegetables you like."

"The banh mi," Emma explained, handing a baguette across the table to Zoe. "So good."

"You guys have such elaborate lunches," Caitlin commented, eyeing with suspicion the vegetables peeking out of the sides of the baguette.

Usually, Zoe loved Uncle Brian's banh mi, which were full of the rich taste of roasted pork and the crisp snap of fresh-pickled vegetables. But she didn't have time to think about food now.

"We got it," she announced breathlessly. "We're doing an advice show!"

"Oh my gosh!" Natalia was so excited, she shot straight up out of her seat, her hands clutching each other. "Congratulations, you guys!" She wrapped her arms around Emma, who was sitting quite still, her cheeks pink and her eyes wide.

"We have to have a whole show ready for next week?" she said in a tight, worried voice.

"It'll be totally fine," Zoe said. "The show is only ten minutes long."

"Ten minutes is longer than you think. We need to get questions," Emma said, frowning in thought. "What if no one writes us with a problem?"

"People love getting advice," Caitlin said. "Don't worry about it, they'll write in." She looked for agreement along the cafeteria table, and the other girls nodded.

"All you need to do is get the word out about your show," Ava said.

"We can make posters tonight and put them up in the halls tomorrow morning," Zoe suggested. In her mind, she could see fun posters in primary colors, eye-catching enough to convince anyone, with any kind of problem, to write in to— "Guys!" she said suddenly. "We need a name for our show."

"What, like *Max and Noah's Sports Talk*?" Natalia asked. "You want to be *Zoe and Emma's Advice Talk*?"

Emma made a face. "I don't like 'Advice Talk,' it sounds weird."

Zoe had a flash of inspiration. "I know," she announced. "How about *Zoe and Emma to the Rescue*? Because we'll be fixing people's problems."

Emma smiled and Zoe knew she was starting to get excited in spite of her nerves.

"*Zoe and Emma to the Rescue*," Emma said, as if trying the name on for size. "I like it!"

Chapter Four

"It's the moment of truth," Zoe said on Sunday afternoon. They'd set up a box in the school library with a slot on the top so that anyone who wanted to could drop in a letter anonymously. She'd taken it home on Friday, so she and Emma could prep for their show. Now Zoe held that box in her lap, and she shook it gently, listening for the sound of paper moving inside. It was hard to tell if there was anything in there, and she exchanged a glance with Emma. Her cousin was nervously twisting her hands together and biting her lip.

Downstairs, she could hear thumping and loud bursts of laughter as Natalia played lava floor with their little brothers.

Had Zoe and Emma inspired anyone to write in with a problem? Would they be able to come to the rescue?

"Here we go," Zoe whispered, a thrill of excitement running down her spine. She couldn't wait any longer. The box top was taped down—so that no one could peek inside—and now she ripped off the tape and threw the box open.

"People wrote in," Emma said faintly, staring down at the pieces of paper inside. "There've got to be fifteen or twenty questions in here. I can't believe it."

"Apparently, we're fabulous," Zoe told her, feeling light-headed with surprise. She couldn't believe it, either. "Okay, I'm going in." She picked up the first note and unfolded it.

Dear Zoe and Emma, My only problem is that I'm so amazing no one can handle it. How can I destroy the haters? PS You guys are laaaammmme.

"Oh," Emma said, disappointed. "It's a fake letter."

"Boys," Zoe said dismissively. Twelve- and thirteen-year-old boys could be amazingly immature, she told herself. It didn't mean anything. But a small knot formed in her stomach. What if they were *all* joke letters?

"Well, let's try another one," she said, trying to sound upbeat.

> *Dear Zoe and Emma, My parents let my older sister get away with everything. They have to know where I am every second, but she gets to go out with her friends as much as she wants. I have to go to bed way before she does, and they are always nagging at me about my homework and grades and how clean my room is, and even when she does way worse than me at school she doesn't get in trouble like I do. It's not fair! Signed, My Parents Like Her Better*

There was a small warm glow in Zoe's chest. This was a real letter. Someone who wanted Emma's and her *help*.

"What do you think?" she asked Emma.

"Some of this is just normal older sibling stuff, right?"

Emma said. "I mean, if her sister's older, of course she gets more freedom and is allowed to stay up later and stuff."

Zoe nodded. "Yeah. I wonder about what she says about them not being fair about the grades thing, though. Do you think it's true? Like, I feel like my parents pick on me and let Natalia get away with stuff sometimes, but it's probably just that it feels like a bigger deal to me when they're mad at *me* or making *me* do something I don't want to, right?"

"I'm sure." Emma laughed. "I don't have a sister, but I think they treat you and Natalia the same."

"But even if they do treat them differently about school, there could be good reasons," Zoe said thoughtfully. "Like, maybe school is more difficult for her sister, and they know she's working really hard. Or she's taking much harder classes. Or maybe the younger one who wrote in has more trouble in school, and their parents keep on top of her to help her."

"How do you know it's a her?" Emma asked, raising her eyebrows.

Zoe read the letter again. "Oh, you're right. I guess I just assumed, because *I* have a sister. It sounds like a girl to me, though."

Emma tucked her feet under her, thinking. "Okay, so what would you say if you were answering the letter?"

Frowning, Zoe looked up at the ceiling as if she might find the right words there. "Well," she said slowly. "I'd point out all the stuff we were just talking about—that older kids do get some freedoms younger kids don't, and that also if she—I mean, she or he—thinks about it, they might see that there are reasons their parents might treat them differently that aren't unfair."

Emma nodded. "Fair doesn't always mean exactly the same."

"Exactly," Zoe said, smiling at her. "That sounds great. But are we just going to tell them their parents are right? What if she—or he, *jeez*—thinks about all that and still feels like their parents aren't being fair? I mean, maybe they're not. Parents aren't always perfect."

There was a thump and a squeal from downstairs, followed by a burst of laughter, and Zoe and Emma exchanged amused looks: Natalia had clearly just fallen into some "lava."

"Okay." Emma brought them back to the question. "What if the parents *aren't* being fair? The kid should talk to them. But not, like, yell at them and accuse them of liking her—*or his*—sister better. Being mad and loud won't make them listen."

Zoe nodded. "And not right in the middle of an argument about homework or bedtimes or whatever. Instead, like, a reasonable conversation when everyone is calm, and maybe the letter writer could just talk about how they *feel* about things instead of making accusations. They could say, 'I feel like Cleopatra doesn't have as much pressure from you about her grades as I do'—and talk about something specific, don't just be like *you're never fair*. And ask: 'Is there a reason you didn't crack down on her like you do on me?'"

"Cleopatra?" Emma asked.

Zoe shrugged. "I needed some kind of name."

Emma smiled. "I think that's a good answer! And this is nice"—she waved a hand back and forth between them—"I like talking about what we think and figuring out an answer together. Maybe we should pick the letters we want to do on the show together and then come up with our own answers and not talk about them till we're doing the show. The show might be more interesting that way. We'd be having this conversation about what we each think on the show."

"Huh." Zoe thought. It did sound like it might be interesting. "But what if we don't agree?"

"So?" Emma said. "We'll talk about what we're thinking. The person will get *two* kinds of advice."

"Okay." Happiness and anticipation were bubbling up inside Zoe. It was going to be a great show, she could feel it. And they had so *many* letters to choose from. "Let's go through and pick two for Wednesday. We can probably do two in ten minutes, right?"

There was another loud thump from downstairs, followed by Abuelita's scolding voice. Emma and Zoe looked at each other again and giggled. Zoe turned back to the letters.

"Okay, we'd better pick two letters before Abuelita breaks up whatever's going on down there and sends Natalia upstairs. She would absolutely get us playing some kind of game, and we'd never figure this out."

Emma ended up staying for dinner. Zoe's dad had cooked, and the big kitchen was fragrant with garlic and spices. Everyone gathered around the table, Zoe next to Emma and across from Natalia and Tomás. Mateo *loved* Emma, and he insisted on sitting on his big cousin's other side.

"My friend Robert wanted to play with the red car first this morning," he told her. "And I was great at sharing and let him instead of grabbing it."

"Good for you," Emma said supportively, handing him a napkin. "You're an excellent sharer."

Zoe looked around the table contentedly. It was dark and cold outside, and the windows rattled when the wind blew. But here, the lamp over the big kitchen table gave a golden light, and everything seemed warm and cozy. Her mom and dad were at one end of the table, talking about the lesson plans her dad was working on for the high school English classes he taught, while Natalia and Tomás, across from Zoe, were quickly and quietly stacking their food into towers, higher and higher, glancing up occasionally to make sure the adults hadn't noticed.

Splat. A lump of Natalia's chicken toppled off its tower and landed on the floor. "Whoops!" she said, and Tomás laughed.

"Kids," their mom said severely, "Stop playing with your food."

"It was *Natalia's* idea!" Tomás said immediately.

"Traitor," Natalia muttered jokingly, and, when her dad looked at her sternly, quickly turned the table's attention to Zoe and Emma. "Hey, how did it go, you guys? Did you get good advice questions?"

"We got *so* many," Zoe said immediately. "And about all kinds of stuff. Friends, parents, brothers and sisters, teachers. Romance, even."

"Sounds like a lot of rich material to work with," their dad said, looking impressed. "You know, it might be a nice activity for my students sometime, writing answers to advice questions."

"More fun than grammar, anyway," Natalia agreed.

Abuelita served Mateo another large spoonful of stir-fry. "Just be careful, girls," she said, shaking her head.

"What do you mean?" Emma said, sounding alarmed.

"Sometimes people ask for advice and they'll take it, especially if the advice they get happens to be the same as what they already want to do," Abuela said. "But if things go wrong for them after they take your advice, they might blame you. Even if it's good advice."

"Don't worry, Abuelita," Zoe said. She sat up straighter, throwing back her shoulders confidently. "No one's going to get mad. We'll be giving *excellent* advice."

Chapter Five

On the next Wednesday morning, the school bus rattled and bounced as it turned down the road toward Waverly Middle School. Zoe held on tightly to the folder in her lap. In it were the two letters they'd chosen to answer today, covered with carefully written notes about how she thought they should be answered. She knew Emma, sitting beside her, had a similar folder in her backpack.

Looking over, she saw that Emma's face was mostly milky pale, with bright spots of pink high on her cheekbones. She was staring fixedly at the back of the bus seat in front of them, and Zoe could see her lips moving slightly. "What are you doing?" she whispered, nudging Emma.

"I'm practicing what I'm going to say," Emma said tightly. "I want it to sound natural."

Zoe wrapped an arm around her cousin and squeezed her into a side hug. She tried to make her voice reassuring, even though her own throat was dry with anxiety. "Relax. It's just going to be us talking about problems people wrote in to us about, like we did at home. There's nothing scary about talking to each other, right? It'll be fun."

"Personally, I can't wait for the show," Natalia said from across the aisle. "Juicy personal problems instead of sports? Yes, *please*! Everyone who's not a total sports nut is going to be *dying* to watch this after a month of playoffs and, um, talking forever about who's going to win what game, or why they didn't win the game. Ugh." She reached over and patted Emma on the knee. "Relax. The only way it could go bad is if you actually fell off your chair. Or I guess if we couldn't hear you guys at all or something. But I'm sure they have microphones. Or, ooh, like, if maybe you threw up." There was a wicked little twinkle in her eye.

"Natalia! Stop it! You're being mean!" Zoe couldn't help laughing.

Emma closed her eyes, shutting Natalia's teasing out. "Game face," she muttered.

The morning announcements were streamed from the student council office on the second floor of the school. As soon as they poked their heads through the door of the office, Charlotte jumped up from where she had been sitting at a long table with several other people and hurried toward them. "Hi!" she said. "Right on time!" She waved a hand at the others around the table. "This is Shoshanna, Mark, Ava, and Oliver."

Everyone said hi, and Zoe smiled at her friend. "We know Ava," she said. "Hey."

"Hi," Emma said. She looked more relaxed now, but Zoe could see how tightly she was holding her bag still, her knuckles white.

"Okay, so, as you know, Oliver and I do the announcements," Charlotte said, speaking very quickly as she waved a hand at the table. "Mark, Ava, and Shoshanna are the crew; they'll figure out any problems you have. Did you bring a script or something?"

"Sort of." Zoe handed her the sheets of questions and notes.

"Okay," Charlotte said, glancing at them. "This is great, but figure out what you want to begin and end on, too. You could do the same thing every week. That way, Shoshanna will know when to turn off the camera. Maybe decide who's going to say what?"

"Sure." Zoe cocked an eyebrow at Emma. "Maybe at the beginning, we can introduce ourselves and say, 'This is *Zoe and Emma to the Rescue*,' and at the end, thank them for watching and say, 'This has been *Zoe and Emma to the Rescue*' again?" She felt awkward repeating the name of the show—*was* it clever, like she'd thought?—but no one seemed to think it was a strange thing to do.

"Sounds good," Emma said. She was standing straighter now, and her knuckles weren't white anymore. Emma, Zoe knew, felt more confident when she was actually *doing* something. It was sitting around thinking about what could go wrong that made her nervous.

"Charlotte, we need to get ready," Oliver called over.

"Okay." Charlotte shot them another gleaming smile. "When Oliver and I finish announcements, we'll get up, and you take our seats at the table and start, okay? If you're not sure about something, Mark will tell you."

She hurried back toward the table, and Ava came over to them.

"Hey!" Zoe said, grinning at her friend. "How's working on the crew going?" Ava had started helping with the morning announcements at the beginning of the week.

"Pretty well," Ava said. "I've learned to use all the equipment, so I'm starting to feel like an old hand at this. Here, let me clip these little microphones to your collars."

As Ava fiddled with the microphones, Zoe looked around with interest. She'd never been in the student council office before. It was so small that there wasn't room for much other than the table and chairs, the digital camera on a tripod that Shoshanna was peering at, long cables connecting it to the computer on a nearby desk, and the seven of them. The walls were covered with brightly colored posters advertising everything from the eighth grade Valentine's dance to the school T-shirt design contest.

"Shh!" Mark said, suddenly, waving everyone in the room to silence. Zoe looked over to see that Charlotte and Oliver were sitting at the table, smiling at the camera. Mark held up three fingers, counting down silently, then pointed to Charlotte and Oliver as Shoshanna zoomed in with the camera.

"Happy Wednesday, Waverly Oysters!" Charlotte shouted happily.

As she and Oliver began the Pledge of Allegiance, Zoe looked through her notes again. Was she sure of her answers to the questions that had come in? Would she sound natural giving them? Beside her, Emma was doing the same thing, frowning thoughtfully.

Charlotte and Oliver's words washed over them, and then suddenly Ava nudged Zoe and pointed to the table.

"And now," Oliver was saying, "our March Wednesday show, *Zoe and Emma to the Rescue.*"

The next minute or two was a blur, and suddenly Zoe found herself sitting behind the table, Shoshanna pointing the camera at her. For a moment, her mouth went dry and her mind went blank. Mark pointed at them.

"Hi!" Emma said suddenly, a fraction too loudly. "We're Emma and Zoe, and this is *Zoe and Emma to the Rescue.*" She paused, and Zoe's mind raced. Was she supposed to say something? How come Emma, who had been so nervous, now seemed totally confident about what she needed to do?

Before Zoe could work out what to say next, Emma went on. "We got some great letters asking for advice. Zoe, do you want to read the first one?"

"Sure," Zoe said. Her mouth was still super-dry, and her voice sounded raspy at first. "Here we go. *Dear Zoe and Emma, How do I get people to stop teasing me? On the first day back from winter break, I slipped and fell off my chair in the cafeteria. My skirt flew up, and I spilled my fruit juice all over my clothes, so I had to walk around with a huge orange stain on my skirt all day.*" Zoe heard her voice get more relaxed as she read. "*Kids in my class are still making fun of me. Sometimes they imitate the look on my face, and how I flailed my arms around as I fell. I try to laugh it off, but my friends tease me about it. I get just as embarrassed every time I think of it as I did when it happened. What should I do?"* Zoe looked up at Emma. "So, what do you think?"

"Wow, that does sound like it was really embarrassing," Emma said. She looked into the camera. "I'm sorry that happened to you. But embarrassing stuff happens to everyone. It's not as big a deal as it might feel like. People think it was funny, but they don't think *you're* dumb or ridiculous. It was just something that happened."

"Yeah," Zoe agreed. "Every single person who teases you, or who even just saw it happen, has had stuff just as embarrassing happen to them. I know *I* have." She shuddered, remembering getting locked in the bathroom backstage at theater club during the intermission of *The Wizard of Oz* and having to shout for help loudly enough that everyone, even the audience, had heard her.

"Sometimes the best thing to do when something embarrassing happens is just to laugh it off," Emma said thoughtfully. "That way, it's still something funny that happened, but you're laughing *with* other people about it, not getting laughed *at*."

"I think that's true, but this is something that happened a whole *month* ago," Zoe said. "Can she suddenly start laughing about it?"

"Why not?" Emma said. "Not, like, hysterical laughter, but when people bring it up, she can just roll her eyes and say, 'Oh, yeah, that was so embarrassing, ha-ha.'"

"She could call them out a little bit about it, too," Zoe said. "Be like, 'Really? You're still talking about this a month later? *Whatever.*' If they realize that it's lame to still be trying to tease someone about something that happened *ages* ago, they might back off."

"I think that laughing it off or being sort of scornful and *whatever* about it will work when people who she isn't close to are the ones teasing her," Emma said. "But it might be worth actually pulling her real friends aside if they're still bringing it up and being like, 'This is upsetting me, I want to forget about it, please stop talking about it.' Because her *real* friends don't want her to feel bad. They might not realize this is something that's hurting her. They probably think she thinks it's kind of funny, too."

"Good point," Zoe said briskly.. She looked into the camera. "So, laugh it off or say *whatever* to people who don't really matter, and try telling your real friends directly that you want them to stop. And remember that embarrassing things happen to everybody and that, in the long run, it's not really a big deal."

"Okay, my turn to read a letter," Emma said. She was smiling, and Zoe grinned, too. The words were coming more easily now. This was starting to be *fun*.

"This is a question about love," Emma went on. "*Dear Zoe and Emma, There's this boy I really, really like. We always smile at each other in class, and my friends think he likes me, too. We haven't talked very much yet, but he seems great. How can I make him see me as more than just a girl in his class?*"

"Ooh, I love this question," Zoe said. "I say do something big and bold to get his attention. It already sounds like you're pretty sure he likes you as much as you like him. So, take the plunge!"

"Like how?" Emma asked, a thin, thoughtful line appearing between her eyebrows.

"Like, some people think that guys should make the first move. But that's ridiculous. Why should they have all the pressure, and all the fun? You should ask *him* out; don't wait around for him to figure it out." Zoe felt like she'd been struck by a bolt of inspiration. "Just go for it! Buy him flowers! Sing him a song! Put a poster on his locker! Make it clear that you like him!"

"Wow, really?" Emma asked. "You think she should put herself out there right away?"

"Absolutely," Zoe said. "What could be more flattering? And it'll be fun. The worst thing that could happen would be that he doesn't like her back, and that's not the end of the world. Better to find out for sure."

"Huh," Emma said slowly. "I agree that she should go ahead and make the first move. But I don't think such a big gesture is a great idea, or that she should ask him out right away. They barely know each other. Maybe she should try *talking* to him. Like, go over and sit with him at lunch. Or ask him if he wants to study together. You need to figure out if you like someone enough to even be friends with them before you start getting all romantic."

"So, we agree that, if you like this guy, you should go ahead and make your move," Zoe said, looking into the camera again. "But whether you take it slow or go with a grand gesture is up to you. Good luck!" Mark was making a "wrap-it-up" gesture. "That's it for this week!" she said.

"Thanks for watching," Emma added. "This has been *Zoe and Emma to the Rescue.*"

Shoshanna smiled and pushed a button on the camera, then Ava clicked the program on the computer to OFF.

"Great job, guys!" she said cheerfully, and the rest of the crew murmured congratulations, too.

"*So* fun!" Charlotte said enthusiastically. "How do you feel?"

Zoe sucked in a deep breath. Her whole body was buzzing with excitement. "I feel *wonderful*," she said.

Chapter Six

"If you feel like your teacher doesn't like you, you should probably start by figuring out why," Zoe said, gazing confidently into the camera. "Do you talk a lot in class, or never do your homework? And maybe you should check with your friends who are in the class to see if *they* think it's true that the teacher specifically doesn't like you. Sometimes I feel like a teacher must hate me, just because I got a bad grade or got in trouble for talking during class or not doing my homework—or because the teacher's a total grouch—but she's not actually treating me any differently than she does anyone else in the same situations."

"If, after all that, you still feel like the teacher's being unfair, you should talk to her," Emma said. "Politely. When you're not mad and she's not mad. Not saying that she doesn't like you, but asking how to improve in her class. Teachers *love* that."

"Or get your parents to talk to her," Zoe added. "Sometimes when you're dealing with grown-ups, you need *your* grown-up on your side." Mark was making his "wrap-it-up" gesture, and she smiled into the camera. "Thanks for watching, and please keep the questions coming!"

"This has been *Zoe and Emma to the Rescue*," Emma finished. "Bye!"

They both grinned at the camera until Shoshanna clicked a button on the camera and stepped back.

"And we're done!" Mark said.

"Good job, guys!" Charlotte said.

Ava, winding up the microphone cords, shot them a thumbs-up, and mouthed, "Thanks!"

Zoe grinned, satisfaction swelling in her chest. The last letter must have been been Ava's! The second show of *Zoe and Emma to the Rescue* had been much easier than the first. And Ava, at least, seemed happy with their advice.

"That was fun," Emma said. She had looked worried before the show—although not as pale and tense as before the first one—but now her cheeks were pink and her eyes were wide with excitement.

"Totally," Zoe agreed. "See? I knew you'd be great at this!"

As they hurried into history, Mr. Thomas stopped handing out papers for a moment and said, "And here are our celebrities!" There was a smattering of applause from the other kids. Emma ducked her head, blushing, but Zoe couldn't stop smiling.

Once they'd settled in their seats and Mr. Thomas had turned back around, a note fluttered over Zoe's shoulder and landed on her desk. Zoe glanced back to see Micah, a skinny boy with glasses, grimacing at her. She unfolded the note.

> Zoe,
>
> I failed my science test and I lied to my parents and said we hadn't gotten them back yet. What do you think I should do?

Zoe blinked. Somebody she knew—not just an anonymous letter writer but someone in her class who was watching her with big, anxious eyes while she read his question—needed her help. Chewing on her lip, she thought for a moment, then scribbled an answer on the same piece of paper.

You have to tell them the truth—they're going to find out anyway. If you go to them and tell them you're having trouble in class and want them to help you figure out how to raise your grade, they won't be as mad as they would be if you didn't tell them. You'll be trying to be responsible!

She folded the paper again and handed it back over her shoulder.

"Zoe!" Mr. Thomas's voice cracked across the room, and Zoe froze. The teacher was looking at her sternly, but all he said was, "Attention on me, please."

Zoe nodded and fixed her eyes on him, pushing Micah's problem to the back of her mind. *I need to forget about advice for a little while.*

But it seemed as if Zoe and Emma's advice show was

at the front of everybody's minds. In math class, she got another two notes passed from different corners of the classroom: one from Colin the basketball star, who wanted to convince his parents to let him get a dog, and one from Lily, who never talked in class, but who wanted to audition for a ballet her dance school was putting on and wasn't sure she could be brave enough.

"It's crazy," she told Emma, flopping down in a seat beside her at the cafeteria table. "Suddenly everyone wants me to run their lives and tell them what to do!"

"I *know*!" Emma said. "People were asking me what I thought about stuff some last week, but now it's gone insane. Diana told me she keeps forgetting her locker combination and asked what kind of memory tricks I know. I mean, that's not really even regular *advice*, is it? Why would I know special memory tricks?"

"We're suddenly experts on everything," Zoe said. "I guess we should enjoy it while it lasts." She reached into her backpack and pulled out a stack of paper. "I brought a bunch of new questions that were in the submissions box. I figured if we went through some every day, we'd be totally ready for next week's show."

"Okay, but let me get out lunch first," Emma said. She opened the boxes in front of her and handed a smaller container to Zoe. "Sushi!"

Louise and Emma's soccer friend Vivian, sitting together on Zoe's other side, wrinkled their noses. "Ugh," Vivian said. "No raw fish for me!"

Zoe cheerfully opened the container and popped a piece of sushi in her mouth. *Delicious.*

Natalia and Caitlin were at the end of the table, their heads close together as they talked. Emma had to reach over and nudge Natalia before she looked up and took her share of the sushi, immediately turning back to Caitlin.

I wonder what they're up to, Zoe thought, but Emma was looking at her expectantly, so she didn't lean over to ask. "Oh!" she said, digging into her backpack and pulling out a few pages. "So, this one's kind of fun," she explained. *"Dear Zoe and Emma, I want to throw a surprise party for my friend's birthday. What's the best way to really surprise her?"*

"Aw, that's so nice!" Emma said. "I'd like to answer a fun one like this after all the serious problems we've been talking about."

Zoe nibbled on a piece of pickled ginger. "Maybe if she threw the party *after* her friend's birthday. If it was like two weeks later, her friend definitely wouldn't be expecting it."

"Yeah, but what if she thinks all her friends have forgotten her birthday?" Emma asked. "She'd be surprised eventually, but she might feel bad on her actual birthday, and I'm sure they don't want that."

"She could have the party a couple weeks *before* her friend's birthday," Louise suggested, leaning across the table. "She won't be expecting that, either."

"That's a good idea," Zoe said, nodding. "Or, if she wanted to throw it close to the actual birthday, they could make other birthday plans—like, say all their friends were going to go to a movie together—and then stop off at somebody's house and make an excuse to go inside. And boom! The party is there."

"Ooh! Or—" Emma began, but suddenly music broke out from the other end of the cafeteria, where the eighth graders sat, interrupting her.

They all turned and craned their necks to stare across the room. Charlotte Avery—upbeat, positive, head-of-the-student-council, super-organizer Charlotte—was *standing on a cafeteria table*, a friend standing on either side, music blasting from speakers at her feet.

"Is this a flash mob?" Ava asked, confused. "Is this what a flash mob is?" As they watched, the girls began to dance, and Charlotte began to sing along with the song.

Charlotte was pointing to the next table.

"Oh my gosh," Natalia said. The boy Charlotte was pointing at was quiet, studious Malcolm Patel, who wrote poems for the school magazine and hardly ever talked. He was gazing up at Charlotte, transfixed, his mouth hanging slightly open.

Charlotte hopped down from the table and walked toward him, still singing.

"I really hope she gets to finish before the lunch ladies stop her," Caitlin said, looking toward where one of the lunchroom aides was making her way through the crowd that had gathered around Charlotte and Malcolm.

The song finished just as Charlotte ended up right in front of Malcolm.

"Malcolm," she said, staring into his eyes, "I really

like you and I think we'd be good together. Would you go out with me?"

There was a long pause. Malcolm's mouth was still hanging open a little.

"Oh no . . ." Emma whispered, twisting her hands together. Zoe could barely breathe. How *awful* for Charlotte if he said no, in front of everybody.

Then Malcolm began to smile. Standing up, he reached out and took Charlotte's hand. "Okay," he said quietly.

Everybody cheered.

"Back to your seats," the lunchroom aide called sternly. "Settle down."

As the crowd that had gathered began to head back to their cafeteria tables, Charlotte and Malcolm, side by side, headed for the cafeteria door.

"Where are they going?" Emma whispered.

"Malcolm has a library pass for lunchtimes," Natalia whispered back. She always seemed to know who had special privileges and who did what when.

As Charlotte and Malcolm passed Zoe's table, Charlotte caught her eye and winked. Zoe smiled back automatically, her breath catching in her throat. *Charlotte* was the one who had written in, asking how to ask a boy out, she realized. Zoe had suggested a big, bold gesture, and Charlotte had taken her advice. And it looked like it actually worked!

That night as she set the table for dinner, Zoe was still flying high on the success of her advice. "I think I have a knack for giving good advice," she told Abuelita as she put out napkins and her grandmother took pork chops out of the oven. "Maybe this is what I'm meant to do. I really feel like I'm helping people, you know?"

"Glad to hear it," Abuelita said cheerfully. "Run up and get your sister and brothers, would you? Dinner's ready."

Upstairs, Mateo and Tomás had a wooden train system sprawling across their bedroom floor and were lying on their stomachs, making *choo-choo* noises and frowning intensely as they pushed little blue-and-red trains along opposite sides of the track. But as soon as Zoe mentioned pork chops, they jumped to their feet and headed for the stairs.

"Don't forget to wash your hands!" she called after them. "Hey, Natalia? Dinner!" There was no reply, and Zoe pushed open the door of Natalia's and her bedroom. "Natalia?"

Natalia was at her desk, bent over something intently, but she jumped when Zoe came in. "What?" she asked, sounding startled, and pushed the papers she'd been looking at into a drawer.

"Dinner," Zoe said again. She came closer, curious. "What are you doing?"

Natalia hesitated. "I'm not ready to talk about it," she said at last. "I'll tell you later, maybe, okay?"

Zoe was immediately *dying* to know what Natalia wasn't telling her, but she listened to her inner advice giver. If she were someone else, she would tell herself to respect her sister's privacy. "Okay," she said. "But definitely tell me later. Because now I'm super-curious."

She was proud of herself, she realized as she slid into her chair, for listening to her *own* good advice and not hassling Natalia to tell her what she was hiding. No wonder everyone wanted to know what she thought they should do about their own problems.

Probably this is my true calling, she thought dreamily. She could imagine getting older and wiser, until huge numbers of people were turning to her, asking her to fix their problems. And she'd be able to do it.

"Okay," older, grown-up, sophisticated big-city Zoe said to the camera. "You've all been writing in with great questions about how to make your lives better, and I'm here to help."

"It's not fair," Mateo said, and the pout in his voice snapped Zoe out of her daydream. "Robert is always grabbing my favorite car. He's a pig!" Her little brother was frowning and glaring at his plate, his arms crossed in front of him.

"Well, honey," their mother began, but Zoe broke in.

"Robert's your friend from school who always has to be first?" she asked, and Mateo nodded. "Why don't you make a deal with him? He can have the red car first every other day, and you get the opposite ones. And you do a big countdown together and then switch halfway through playtime."

"Center time," Mateo corrected her. "We both like the car center."

"Okay," Zoe said. "But if you make it into a game—a *sharing* game—instead of fighting over the car, he might be more likely to go along with it."

Mateo thought it over and then uncrossed his arms and picked up his fork, looking less pouty. "Okay, I'll try," he said. Zoe smiled and slipped back into her daydream.

"The most important thing is to understand the other person's psychology," grown-up Zoe told her fans. "Get people on your side, so they want the same thing you do."

Grown-up artist/advice-giving celebrity Zoe was untangling a complicated romantic problem from a fan when the sound of another voice interrupted her.

"The guests look at this amazing food Brian's made for them, and they decide suddenly, without bothering to tell us in advance, that they won't eat anything with tomatoes, and that everything has to be carb-free," Zoe's mom was saying to her dad and Abuelita. "We can't fix a brand-new dish every time we get a fussy eater, or we're going to go broke."

"Well, why don't you have them fill out their food preference online when they register?" Zoe suggested. "If they've had a chance to tell you about all their special diet stuff, Uncle Brian will have time to figure out in advance what everybody might be willing to eat."

Her mom blinked. "I should have thought of that," she said. "Thanks, Zoe, that's smart advice."

"You just think you're an expert on everything now, don't you?" Natalia said wryly, but she was smiling.

Zoe looked down modestly, but she couldn't help feeling smug. *Well, I kind of am.*

Chapter Seven

The whole next week went by the same way. Every day, kids came up to Zoe and told her how great the show was, or asked Emma and her to give advice on their problems. All kinds of problems: She found herself trying to think of good ideas for what to enter in an art exhibit and what kind of birthday cake was best. Even the silliest questions filled her with a fizzing, excited joy—what she said *mattered*, it was *important*; she was helping people to solve problems they couldn't solve themselves.

Even when they didn't directly ask her, Zoe felt like good ideas to fix people's problems were just popping out of her mouth without her even trying hard. She heard Vivian complaining about her grade on a math test, and suggested asking for a tutor; she heard Alice, who she knew from theater club, saying that she was sick of the dinners her mom cooked, and slipped her a couple of Uncle Brian's best recipes to share with her mom.

Wednesday, Zoe watched as Oliver and Charlotte went through the Pledge of Allegiance and the morning announcements—a PTA bake sale, chorus auditions, the school T-shirt contest—and stood still as Ava threaded the microphone through her collar, and exchanged a smile with Emma as they took their seats behind the table, all with a buoyant sense of *rightness*. This was something she was good at, and something she really liked.

Charlotte winked at her again as she passed them, and Zoe felt a little glow of pride, deep in her chest. Charlotte and Malcolm had been holding hands in the halls all week: Zoe's advice had been a stroke of genius.

"We've got two great questions for you today," she said brightly, after she and Emma had opened the show and introduced themselves. "And they're both about trouble with friends."

Emma read the first one. *"Dear Zoe and Emma, I have four really good friends; we've known each other since* kindergarten and we all hang out together a lot. My parents let me have a slumber party, but they only let me invite three of my friends—they said we just didn't have room for another girl. I tried to keep the party secret from the friend I couldn't invite, but she found out, and now she's mad at me. I still want to be friends! What should I do?"

"Ugh," Zoe said, grimacing. "This has definitely happened to me, both having to leave somebody out and being the one who's left out. A couple years ago, my twin sister got invited to a party a friend of both of ours was having, and I didn't. That was totally devastating."

"I'm sure," Emma said. "But, like you said, I've been on the other side of that, too. I had a birthday party at a craft store last year, and they had a maximum number of people I could invite, so I had to leave out some of my friends. I felt terrible about it."

Zoe looked into the camera. "Everybody understands that sometimes there isn't room for everyone we'd like to invite, and I'm sure your friend gets that you couldn't invite as many people as you wanted to. But the truth is that, when you had to choose someone to leave out, you chose her."

Emma nodded. "And that's what she's *really* upset about. Like, the slumber party would have been fun, but the real issue is that now she feels like she's not as good a friend of yours as the other girls are."

"So how can you fix it?" Zoe asked. "I'm assuming you've explained what happened, that your parents made you leave someone out, but I think you need to do something to show her that she's important to you."

"Maybe you could take her somewhere, just the two of you," Emma suggested. "Like out for cupcakes, or to do something fun, like ice skating. Or have a sleepover that's only you two."

"Those are awesome ideas," Zoe said. "Another thing you could do is give her a letter or a card where you let her know that you didn't want to hurt her feelings. Tell her that her friendship is important to you. I think actually writing down, in a thoughtful way, how you feel and that you care, can make a big impression."

"Because that's probably what she wants to know," Emma agreed. "That you care."

"Okay, moving on," Zoe said. She looked down at the printout of the next question they'd chosen and read,

"Dear Zoe and Emma, My BFF is working on something to enter into a contest. She's really creative and smart, but her project just isn't that good. She keeps asking me what I think, and I've tried to be sort of neutral and not make her feel bad, but she keeps coming back and wanting detailed opinions from me. I don't want to be mean to her, but I feel like she's going to get all excited and then be really disappointed— there's no way she's going to win the contest with this project. I'd hate to see her get her feelings hurt. Should I tell her the truth?"

"Huh." Emma frowned thoughtfully. "Actually, I think this is a situation where telling the truth isn't going to do any good, unless you have specific suggestions that might help. Like, I wouldn't tell her that what she's doing is amazing, but why make your friend feel bad? You're not one of the judges. They might feel differently about her project."

Zoe shook her head. "I totally disagree," she said. "She's your friend and she's asking for your opinion. You *owe* it to her to be honest with her. She deserves to know the truth. You should be really direct. She'd probably rather hear it from you than from the judges."

Emma shrugged. "I don't think you should crush your friend's hopes. Let her try without discouraging her."

"I guess this is one question where we're just going to have different opinions," Zoe said. She looked into the camera again. "Maybe think about our two answers and follow the one that makes sense to you? This has been *Zoe and Emma to the Rescue.* Thanks for watching."

Once the camera was off and the microphones were unclipped, Zoe followed Emma and Ava down the hall toward first period. The show had been fun, just as it had the first two times. But Zoe felt a tiny bit of unease, as if something cold was trickling slowly down her back. Even though they sometimes had different points of view, Emma and Zoe had never *completely* disagreed on an answer before. What if Emma was right and Zoe was wrong?

Nah, Zoe reassured herself. *Emma is just too cautious sometimes. She worries too much about hurting people's feelings. Honesty is always the best policy, right?*

After all, Zoe had a natural gift for giving advice. She was sure of it.

As usual, the cafeteria was loud: a babble of a hundred conversations and bursts of laughter, trays slamming down on tables, chairs squeaking against the floor. Zoe slipped into a seat at their usual table. Emma and Natalia were already there, Emma unpacking tiny individual quiches from her extra-large lunch bag. She handed one across the table to Zoe.

"Is there bacon in this?" Zoe said curiously, poking at it with her fork.

Natalia had already bitten into hers, and she frowned thoughtfully. "I think I taste Swiss cheese, too," she said.

Zoe thought it might actually be Muenster and was about to say so when a familiar voice rose above the others, catching her attention.

"It's not fair." Charlotte and Malcolm were standing in a corner near the edge of the cafeteria, glaring at each other. Charlotte's voice was bitter.

"Don't be like that," Malcolm said, running a hand through his hair. "I don't *want* to hang out with your friends all the time. I need to be by myself, to think. I'm trying to come up with a whole science fiction universe."

"But what's the point of even going out if you never want to spend any time together?" Charlotte said. Her bottom lip was pushed out, and her voice trembled.

"Fine," Malcolm said, but he sounded resentful, as if he didn't actually agree with her. Grabbing Charlotte's hand, he pulled her toward the eighth-grade tables.

Zoe stared after them, troubled. The trickling feeling of dread had returned. Charlotte had followed Zoe's advice and it had worked—Malcolm liked her, too, and now they were going out. But they sure didn't look happy anymore.

Every couple fights, Zoe told herself. *They'll be fine.*

But what if they weren't? Zoe couldn't help wondering, what if her advice had been wrong? If Charlotte and Malcolm were unhappy, was it *her* fault?

Chapter Eight

"I don't think you need to worry about it," Natalia chirped, bouncing a little in the bus seat across the aisle from Zoe and Emma. "From what I hear, Malcolm and Charlotte are going strong. They were holding hands when they left school."

Beside her, Caitlin shook her head. "I don't know," she said. "I don't think they have a lot in common. Charlotte's so perky and Malcolm's all quiet and mysterious."

Natalia rolled her eyes. "That's the point," she told Caitlin. "Didn't you ever hear that opposites attract?"

"Anyway, Malcolm and Charlotte are not your problem," Emma said sensibly. "Charlotte chose to go after Malcolm, and either things will work out between them or they won't. Not every couple lasts forever, especially in middle school."

Zoe sighed. Charlotte and Malcolm never would have gotten together if it hadn't been for her. "Giving people advice is a real responsibility," she said. Natalia and Caitlin glanced at each other, smirking, and Zoe stiffened. "Well, it *is*."

"Okay, then," Natalia said mildly. The bus was coming up to their stop, and she and Caitlin started gathering up their stuff. "Are you guys coming?"

Zoe shook her head. "Tell Mom I'm at Emma's and I'll be back for dinner, okay? Caitlin, you're staying for dinner at our place, right? I'll see you later."

"Okay," Natalia said amiably, and Caitlin waved good-bye.

Zoe watched as her twin and Caitlin climbed off the bus, and then turned to Emma. "So, you think Charlotte and Malcolm are okay?"

Emma sighed. "Like I said, whether they are or not, I don't think it's your fault, Zoe. You're getting kind of obsessive about this."

"I guess." The bus rattled to a stop at Emma's corner, and the girls grabbed their backpacks and climbed off. As they headed for Seaview House, Zoe tried to explain.

"I really like giving advice," she told Emma, who nodded in agreement. "But if the advice I'm giving isn't good, aren't I hurting people?"

They walked across the lawn to Seaview House without talking much, frost-covered grass crunching under their feet. Spring was coming, every day a little warmer than the last, but it was still so cold at night. Zoe huddled more deeply into her jacket.

"Well, they don't have to take our advice," Emma said at last, as they pushed open the front door of the bed-and-breakfast. "We just have to do the best we can."

The warmth of the inn felt like a welcoming embrace after the cold outside. The stained glass–shaded lamps by the couches in the front room were lit against the darkening afternoon, and they gave a rosy, peaceful glow to the whole room. The B and B guests were doubtless all out and about in town, but Zoe could hear Emma's dad chopping something in the kitchen.

Grandma Stephenson was tidying the living room, reshelving books that guests had pulled out of the bookcases. She turned when they came in and smiled. "Two of my favorite granddaughters," she said, and Zoe and Emma hurried over to hug her.

"I haven't seen you for almost a week, sweetheart. You were at brunch, but I didn't get a chance to talk to you," she said, smoothing Zoe's hair back from her forehead. She peered into Zoe's face questioningly, her eyes the same shade of light blue as Emma's. "You look a little tired. Are you getting enough sleep?"

"Sure," Zoe said. "Just a long day at school."

"I see," Grandma Stephenson said, her gaze sharp. "Well, I'm sure Emma will cheer you up."

Emma grinned. "Naturally."

"But first," Grandma went on, "I suggest we repair to the kitchen. Your father"—she looked at Emma—"has spent the day experimenting with new cookie recipes. He'll need our help to test them."

"Well," Zoe said, considering, "if it's to help the family business." She pushed away the worried, tight feeling she'd been carrying around since she saw Charlotte and Malcolm arguing in the cafeteria. She was here, in the house her family had lived in for generations, people she loved all around her, and she could smell the lingering scent of baking cookies now. Those worries might hover at the back of her mind, but what could she do about Charlotte and Malcolm now? She might as well eat cookies.

⚭

"Ugh, I'm still so full," Zoe said an hour later, flopping down on Emma's bed. The cookies had been terrific: crispy light ginger biscuits, rich shortbreads, and refreshing tiny bites filled with lemon curd. She and Emma had been able to weigh in with total confidence that Uncle Brian should add them all to the afternoon tea hour for guests. But they'd eaten way too many.

After they'd eaten as many cookies as they could possibly hold, Zoe had painted a last few details on Hatshepsut's cardboard sarcophagus, which was due the next day—the oral report was all prepared—and they'd gone through some advice questions. It looked like Caitlin had gone back over Natalia's constructions, neatening the corners of the sarcophagus and brushing gold paint around the edges of the tomb itself. It was *exactly* like Caitlin, Zoe thought, to go back and adjust other people's work to fit her standards, but Zoe had to admit it looked good. Now she had the comfortable feeling of having met all her responsibilities and having the rest of the afternoon and night guiltlessly free.

"I still think maybe we should pick the question about the parents getting divorced," Emma said, sitting next to Zoe's feet and leaning back against the wall. "It's a really important thing to deal with."

"Yeah," Zoe agreed. "But I'm not sure how much advice we can give. Like, talk to your friends, talk to your parents, remember it's not your fault. Parents getting divorced isn't something kids can do much about; they just kind of have to deal with it."

"I guess." Emma twisted her fingers together. "Still, it's our last show next week. I want to do something really worthwhile."

"We will," Zoe said. She didn't like to think about the show ending and somebody new taking their place. Eager to change the subject, she rolled over on the bed to gaze out of Emma's windows.

Emma's parents had made a cozy apartment out of part of the attic when they'd been renovating Seaview

House so that they and Emma would have a space a little separate from the rest of the B and B. One whole side of Emma's sloping-ceilinged bedroom was windows, looking out over Seaview House's rose gardens and down to the Chesapeake Bay. In the summer, it was beautiful, full of the sweet fragrance rising up from the garden and with a view of the bay all blue and white and alive with boats. But now the roses were dormant, their bushes looking like just bundles of gray-and-brown sticks, while the bay was nearly empty of boats and reflected the heavy gray of the sky.

"It's kind of bleak-looking out there," Zoe observed.

Emma wrinkled her nose. "I know," she said. "My room was really nice before it got all cold and dismal out, but now it's pretty depressing. I can't wait for summer to get here."

Zoe looked around. She and Natalia had helped Emma decorate her room when their cousin and her family had first moved into Seaview House. It was all done in shades of blue and white, vaguely nautical looking. A hammock swung in one corner, piled high with cushions. When the sun had been shining and the bay had been blue, Emma's room had felt like an extension of the outdoors, like summer. Now the cool, watery colors made everything feel chilly.

But Zoe could imagine the refreshing early spring version of this room. "All you need is some new colors," she told Emma. "Maybe a light green. Or yellow or pink." In her mind's eye, she could see soft spring colors covering every surface, giving the high-up little room the feeling of a spring garden.

Emma looked doubtful. "Pink and yellow together?" she asked. "Won't it look kind of like a baby shower or something?"

"Wait and see," Zoe said, scrambling off the bed and onto her feet. "I bet we can find stuff in the rest of the attic." The top floor of Seaview House was mostly a sprawling storage space full of boxes and chests and old furniture, ranging from the boxes of Christmas ornaments tucked away two months ago to trunks that had belonged to their ancestors more than a hundred years before. Stephensons apparently never threw anything away.

"Look at *this*," Zoe said exultantly, a couple hours later. They'd found a lot of treasure in the attic: fluffy sunshine-yellow curtains and pillow covers covered in a pattern of twining vines and flowers, which Emma's mom had been happy to let them have. They'd run the material through the washing machine to get rid of dust. The real find, though, had been a great carved trunk full to the brim with different fabrics. Grandma had said that it had probably belonged to her own aunt, who had made all of her own clothes and been "a bit dramatic."

The fabrics were pretty dramatic, that was for sure. Zoe and Emma had tacked up swaths of shimmering silk in different shades of green, and Zoe had managed to fasten a huge piece of pink silk across the ceiling, where it billowed like a cloud.

"It looks amazing," Emma agreed. She and Zoe grinned proudly at each other. The room wasn't cold and bleak anymore at all—it reminded her of a bird's nest, perched high in a flowering country garden. Or an Impressionist painting, romantic and beautiful. Magical.

Maybe I should be an interior decorator, she thought: *A cool one who's very artistic.*

She could picture it:

> *Grown-up city Zoe listened patiently as a client asked for help. Her living room was bland and dismal: Coming home didn't make her happy. But Zoe knew just what to do. Soon she had a paintbrush in her hand and was climbing a ladder, painting murals on the walls of the unlivable living room. High white birch trees stretched up the walls, their branches reaching across a ceiling painted with a twilight sky.*
>
> *"This is perfect," her client gasped. "Now my house is finally a home. And thank you for your advice on my family's problems as well. You've fixed my life and my living room."*

It was all part of the same thing, wasn't it? Zoe thought. She could help people by giving them good advice on their problems, or by making their spaces beautiful. Emma was happier now because of Zoe, and so were a lot of the people she'd given advice to. *Maybe I'll be a therapist or an interior decorator or have my own show when I grow up*, Zoe thought, *as well as being an artist.*

Walking home through the dusk, Zoe felt buoyant with pride at how great Emma's room had looked. She was still worried, though, about the kid who had written in about their parents' divorce. They hadn't been able to help with that question, but Zoe thought what she'd told Emma had been right: With some problems, there just wasn't anything they could do to make a situation better.

Nevertheless, though, this had been a good afternoon. The warm, light sensation in her chest now was the same as the feeling she got when she came up with a really good solution to someone's problem. She'd used her creativity to *help* Emma, and Emma had loved it.

It was even colder out now than it had been when they went to Seaview House, and Zoe balled her gloved hands up in her coat pockets to keep her fingers warm. She walked faster as she came in sight of her own house.

The windows were glowing from the lights inside, golden and welcoming, and her stomach growled as she wondered what they'd be having for dinner. She was coming home later than she'd planned, and dinner must be almost ready.

Just as Zoe reached the steps up to the front door, the door opened and then slammed behind a hurrying figure.

"Caitlin?" Zoe asked, as the other girl rushed down the steps. "Aren't you staying for dinner?"

Close up, she saw that Caitlin's eyes were shiny with suppressed tears and her mouth was in a thin, angry line. "Are you okay?" Zoe asked.

"No," Caitlin said bitterly. "I never should have taken *your* advice, Zoe."

"Huh?" Zoe asked, puzzled. "What do you mean?" She took hold of Caitlin's arm to make the other girl look at her, but Caitlin pulled away as a car came slowly down the street toward them.

"That's my dad," she said. "I've got to go." Her shoulders were stiff and defensive-looking, even from behind, as she hurried to her dad's car and got in, shutting the door behind her.

What was that about? Zoe suddenly felt anxious and apprehensive: When had Caitlin taken *her* advice? Was she almost crying because of Natalia? What had happened? Her stomach hollow with dread, she ran up the front steps and into the house, then straight upstairs to the bedroom she and Natalia shared.

Natalia was curled up on the bed. When she looked up at Zoe, tears were running down her face.

"Oh no," Zoe said, rushing over to her sister and sitting on the bed beside her. "What's wrong?"

Natalia sniffed and sat up, wiping her face on her arm. "Caitlin was being really mean to me," she muttered. "She's so harsh sometimes."

"What *happened*?" Zoe asked. Caitlin could be insensitive sometimes, sure—she had been pretty unfriendly to Emma when Emma first moved to Waverly, for instance—but she and Natalia were solid best friends. Zoe couldn't imagine Caitlin being mean to Natalia on purpose.

Natalia huffed a sigh. "I guess I might as well tell you," she said. "I've been working on an entry for the school T-shirt contest."

"Okay," Zoe said, remembering how Natalia had hurriedly hidden papers when Zoe came into the room. "Great. But why were you keeping that a secret?" She tried not to sound hurt; Natalia was upset enough.

Natalia dropped her head onto her knees. "It's just that you're better at art than I am," she said, her voice muffled. "I was kind of embarrassed to show you, because I know my art isn't that good, but I was excited about my idea. So, I kept asking Caitlin what she thought of it, and she was always like, 'Why do you want to know what I think? It's what you think that matters.'" She raised her head and looked at Zoe through a curtain of hair. "But I just wanted her opinion. So, today, when I asked again, she told me exactly what she thought of my entry for the T-shirt contest, and she was *mean* about it. She was like, 'I'm sorry, but I don't think it's any good. I think you might be embarrassed if you enter it.'"

"Wow," Zoe said. "That *is* pretty harsh." An uneasy tendril of guilt was creeping through her. Caitlin had said she never should have taken Zoe's advice. It must have been *Caitlin* who had written in to the show, and Zoe had told her to be honest and bold, to tell the truth instead of worrying about her friend's feelings.

Zoe twisted her hands in her lap. "I'm sure Caitlin was just trying to be honest and it came out wrong."

"There's a difference between *honest* and *mean*," she said. Dropping her head back, she stared up at the ceiling. "So, then I told her she was totally insensitive, and *she* got all upset and said I shouldn't have nagged her for her opinion if I didn't want to hear it, and we were both furious. Now I'm just really embarrassed. I don't even want to see Caitlin for a while."

Caitlin's a pretty blunt person. She probably didn't mean to hurt Natalia's feelings. Zoe still wasn't convinced that the trouble between Natalia and Caitlin wasn't mostly her own fault but decided to focus on the immediate problem. "Will you show me the T-shirt design now? Maybe I can help you."

"I might be too embarrassed to even be able to show you. You're really arty, and Caitlin made it clear just how bad it was," Natalia said reluctantly, turning her face away.

"Oh, come on." Zoe nudged her sister. "I'm your *twin*. We dressed as peanut butter and jelly for a joint Halloween costume when we were eight. You read the poetry I wrote to the boy I was in love with in fourth grade. If you can't show me embarrassing stuff, who can you show it to?"

"I guess." Natalia's cheeks were faintly pink, but she got up and pulled a paper out of her desk drawer. "See?" she said. "I thought the pearl thing would be nice, because we're the Waverly Oysters."

Zoe looked at the paper her sister had handed her. Drawn on it in black marker was a pair of ovals that she guessed were supposed to be an open oyster. Inside stood a couple of smiling stick figures, a large circle between them. Above, it read: *Waverly Middle School: A Pearl of a School.*

"Caitlin's right, isn't she?" Natalia said miserably. "It's awful."

"I don't think it's awful," Zoe said. It really wasn't. There was definitely potential in her sister's idea— maybe it was because they were twins, but Zoe felt like she could see past the roughness of the drawing to the way Natalia had seen the design in her head, and that design was pretty cool looking. "Okay, your drawing isn't great, but I think the pearl slogan is really cute for the Oysters. And the composition is nice and clean. You didn't put too much stuff in the picture, and the eye is drawn right to the pearl. Does it have to be in black and white?"

Natalia nodded. "The rules said the T-shirts were going to be black print on white shirts."

"Okay." Zoe could picture the shirts in shades of ocean blue and sunset pink, which would look much cooler than black and white, but the rules were the rules. She looked at Natalia's drawing again. If it was a little clearer that the ovals were an oyster shell . . . If the two stick figures were a little more elaborate and it was clear that one was a girl and one a boy . . . A little shading might make it more obvious that the circle was a pearl.

"I really like your idea," she said hesitantly, unsure how Natalia would take her suggestion. "But the art is kind of messy. What if I helped with the art, just adapting the images and using the slogan you came up with? We could enter together."

Natalia bit her lip. "I knew my art wasn't good enough," she said.

"But your *ideas* are good," Zoe said. "And if you actually want to get better at drawing, you can take a class. Drawing's just like anything else: You get better with practice."

Natalia wrinkled her nose, then suddenly grinned. "I don't actually want to put any work into being a good artist," she admitted. "It's not that important to me. You can be the family artist. But I really like my idea for the T-shirt and I want it to turn out the way I pictured it."

Zoe smiled back and picked up a pencil from Natalia's desk. "So," she said, twirling the pencil between her fingers, "we're sisters. Let me help."

Chapter Nine

The next morning, Zoe pushed open the front door of the school and held it open so that Natalia and Emma could carefully carry in the tomb of Hatshepsut they were presenting as part of their history project. Zoe and Natalia's dad had given them a ride to school so they wouldn't have to wrestle their project on and off the bus. They ended up being a little earlier than usual this morning, because he had to get over to the high school before his own classes began.

Zoe looked proudly at the tomb as Emma and Natalia carried it past her through the door. She thought it looked pretty impressive. Natalia had done the base building, cleverly fitting bits of different cardboard boxes together to make an almost waist-high room with one open side to see into and a curving ceiling like that of the real Hatshepsut's tomb. She'd given everything a smooth background coat of creamy paint.

Zoe had precisely and elaborately painted all the sides and even the ceiling with hieroglyphics and frescoes of stiffly posed, white-clad Egyptian deities, copied from the pictures they'd found online of the female pharaoh's real tomb. In the center of the room was a topless box, made of cardboard painted to look like stone, and inside that was the mummy case. Zoe had painted that very carefully, trying to replicate the knowing, secretive smile on the real outer mummy case of the female pharaoh.

Emma and Caitlin had, after some discussion with the twins, written up the oral reports they'd be giving together. Emma was going to talk about government in ancient Egypt, and Caitlin was going to talk about the female pharaoh Hatshepsut and the role women in general played in ancient Egypt. Natalia would talk about pyramids and how they were built, and Zoe would talk about the art inside the pyramids, what the different conventions were and what they symbolized to the ancient Egyptians.

As her sister and cousin carried the tomb into the history classroom, Zoe suddenly remembered she'd left the script for her part of the presentation in her locker. "I'll be right back, you guys," she called as she headed down the hall.

She was standing at her locker, reading through the presentation, when she heard a throat being cleared behind her.

"Hey," Caitlin said, when Zoe turned around.

"Hey," Zoe answered. "We brought the tomb in."

Caitlin nodded. "Is Natalia still mad at me?" she asked. Her voice sounded slightly hoarse, as if she was coming down with a cold. She was looking tired. There were dark circles under her eyes, and Zoe thought she looked like she probably hadn't slept well.

"Yeah, kind of," Zoe said. There was no point in lying, but she felt bad when she saw Caitlin's shoulders get tight and defensively high. "I think she's mostly just embarrassed," Zoe added apologetically.

"I didn't do anything wrong," Caitlin insisted, her chin beginning to jut out. "She kept *asking* me what I thought. And *you* told me to tell her the truth."

"Well, yeah," Zoe admitted. "And I still think it was a good thing that you did. She and I worked on revising the T-shirt design, and it's way better now. And we wouldn't have worked together on it if you hadn't given her some criticism."

Caitlin's shoulders slumped. "Well, then, why is she still mad at me?" she said plaintively.

"You hurt her feelings," Zoe explained. "Maybe if you apologized?"

Caitlin sniffed. "I don't really think I have anything to apologize *about*. But fine, if it'll make her happy."

Zoe closed her locker, and they headed back to the classroom together. Caitlin was stomping along, her boots clomping angrily on the hall floor

"Um," Zoe said. "You don't *have* to apologize."

Caitlin huffed in a breath, then sighed. "No, if Natalia feels bad, I don't want her to be upset."

Zoe followed Caitlin into the classroom, where Natalia and Emma were bending over the tomb, doing a couple last-minute adjustments. Natalia was frowning a little as she fiddled with the edge of the sarcophagus. A few other kids had trickled into the room now, too, and were talking or flipping through books or resting their heads on their desks sleepily. Mr. Thomas's chair was empty, though. He was probably just in the teacher's lounge, getting coffee.

"The roof got bent a little bit," Emma explained, looking up at Zoe and Caitlin. "But we fixed it."

"Great," Zoe said. Her stomach twisted. Natalia looked kind of mad. Zoe just wanted them all to be friends again.

Caitlin walked straight up to Natalia, her head held high. "I want to apologize," she said quietly.

"Okay," Natalia said. There was a hopeful tilt to her face. Zoe could tell her sister didn't *want* to be mad at Caitlin; she was sure they both just wanted to go back to things being normal.

"I didn't mean to hurt your feelings," Caitlin said. "I didn't know you were going to be so sensitive about the T-shirt drawing." Behind Natalia and Caitlin, Zoe saw Emma silently facepalm.

Natalia stiffened. "I *wasn't* being too sensitive," she snapped. "*You* were being mean."

"That's not true," Caitlin said sharply. "You *asked*

me what I thought. Over and over again. I even said I liked the idea, but you kept pestering me about the drawing."

Their voices were rising, and Zoe realized that the rest of the kids in the class were listening with interest. "Guys . . ." she said.

"I asked Zoe what she thought, too," Natalia said. "And she didn't tell me how horrible it was. She *helped* me."

"Yeah, well, Zoe helped me, too, when I wrote in asking what to do about you. She was the one who told me to be honest. Apparently, it wasn't actually all that helpful advice." Natalia and Caitlin were glaring at each other now, their hands on their hips.

"Hey," Zoe objected, beginning to get angry herself. "I told you to be honest, but I didn't tell you to be totally tactless. Don't drag *me* into your fight."

"You guys, calm down," Emma said, anxiously twisting her hands together.

"Wait, you wrote to Zoe and Emma's advice show about how bad my project was?" Natalia asked, taken aback. "That was about me?"

Caitlin bit her lip, looking guilty. "It wasn't about how bad—"

"Thanks a lot, Caitlin," Natalia said bitterly. "That's just really embarrassing."

"Oh, for heaven's sake," Caitlin snapped. "It's just a T-shirt. Stop being such a baby."

There was a ripple of laughter from some of the boys in the class.

Natalia gasped. She looked *furious*. Suddenly, her mouth dropped open farther, and she glared at Caitlin.

"I just figured something out," she said in a low voice. "I was thinking that the sarcophagus didn't look quite the way it did when I put it together. Did you go back and change it?"

Caitlin's eyes widened. "I just neatened it up a little," she said. "You left some of the corners kind of raggedy. I always touch stuff up, you know that."

Natalia looked ready to scream in anger and frustration. Before she could speak, though, Mr. Thomas walked through the door, holding a full cup of coffee, and seemed to take in the tension between them in a glance. "Settle down, kids," he said firmly. "Girls, are you all set to start your presentation?"

Caitlin and Natalia were still glaring silently at each other. After a moment, Zoe said, "Sure," and Emma nodded.

Mr. Thomas sat down at his desk and gestured to them to begin.

"Um, okay," Emma said, looking down at her notes. Zoe felt a wave of relief that Emma's part was first, instead of one of the others'. Beside her, Caitlin's jaw was clenched tightly, and Natalia was looking like she might cry, or throw something at Caitlin. And *Zoe* certainly didn't want to go first.

"Ancient Egypt was governed by the pharaohs," Emma read. "The pharaohs were the heads of the religion, as well as the heads of the government. Officially, people believed that they were half human and half god."

As Emma went on, Zoe looked around the classroom. Some of the kids were smirking at Natalia and Caitlin— there were always kids who loved drama—and others looked kind of worried. Natalia and Caitlin had been best friends for years.

Emma finished her part of the speech, and there was a short, awkward pause. Zoe looked over at Caitlin, who was supposed to go next, but Caitlin was staring off into space, frowning.

Zoe nudged her, and Caitlin jumped. "Women in ancient Egypt had the same rights under the law as men did," she said in a rushed, angry-sounding voice, and then she looked down at her paper for another silent minute, clearly finding her place, before she continued in a more level voice.

When Caitlin finished, it was Natalia's turn.

She began right away. "The oldest known pyramid in Egypt," she said, her voice wobbling a little, "was built around the year 2630 BC . . ." Her voice trailed off, and the paper shook slightly in her hand.

Suddenly, Zoe realized her sister was struggling not to cry. Slipping closer to her, Zoe looked over Natalia's shoulder at the paper. "The last major pyramid was built around 664 BC," Zoe read aloud. She pressed her arm gently against Natalia's, trying to reassure her.

Zoe could hear Natalia sniffing a little, but her hands had steadied, and she didn't seem like she was about to cry anymore. After a deep breath, she spoke up again, her voice more confident than before. Zoe and Emma exchanged a relieved glance.

"What a horrible morning," Zoe muttered quietly to Emma as they came into the cafeteria together.

Caitlin and Natalia were sitting at opposite ends of the lunch table. Both girls looked up at them expectantly as they approached. Zoe realized she and Emma were going to have to make a choice about who to sit with.

Well, Natalia's my sister, she thought. *I have to be loyal to her. It's a no-brainer.* She plopped down next to Natalia, and Emma sat down beside her and began to open her lunch bag. "Brie and pear sandwiches today," she said with false brightness. "And some of those lemon curd cookies from the B and B, yum."

"Sounds good," Zoe said, looking over at Caitlin at the other end of the table. She was sitting a little separately from everyone else, and now she was staring down at her own lunch, her lips tight.

Most of these girls are really Natalia's friends, she realized. *Caitlin gets along with them fine, but they'd choose*

Natalia's side if they had to choose. Natalia was so friendly; people flocked to her. Caitlin was a little more private. Zoe felt bad: Caitlin had been tactless, but she hadn't meant to be mean. She shouldn't have to sit by herself.

"You should talk to her," she said softly to Natalia. "You've been friends for so long, and she was only trying to help."

Natalia shook her head, her lips tight. Zoe and Emma exchanged a look.

"Well . . ." Emma said.

She trailed off as a loud, angry voice said: "You're nothing like I thought you were!"

In the middle of the cafeteria, Charlotte and Malcolm were glaring at each other. A hush fell over the rest of the room as everyone turned to look at them curiously.

"Well, you're nothing like I thought you'd be, either!" Malcolm—quiet, introverted Malcolm—shouted back. "If I had known how shallow and hyper you are, I never would have wanted to go out with you."

"Oh, yeah?" Charlotte growled, her fists clenching. "Well, I think you're boring! And selfish! I thought you were mysterious, but now I've realized that maybe you just don't have anything to say!"

Malcolm yanked a woven bracelet off his wrist. "You can have your friendship bracelet back," he said. "It looks tacky anyway."

Charlotte grabbed the bracelet out of his hand. "I'd be really offended by that, if I thought you had any idea what looks good. If I had known what you were really like, I *never* would have asked you out." Turning her back on him, she stormed away.

Malcolm stared after her for a moment, and then he stalked off in the opposite direction, toward the doors out of the cafeteria.

There were a few seconds of silence, and then a buzz of excited conversation burst out all over the cafeteria. Zoe pushed her sandwich out of the way and dropped her head down onto the table.

"It's official," she moaned. "I give terrible, terrible advice." Rolling her head to the side, Zoe looked up at Emma. "Charlotte should have listened to you," she said sadly. "You told her to get to know Malcolm as a friend before she made any kind of move. She could have found out whether or not she actually liked him before they started going out."

"Actually, I think your advice was pretty good," Emma said reassuringly. Zoe snorted. "No, listen. She wanted to know how to get Malcolm interested in her, right? Well, your suggestion worked perfectly. She made a big move and really got his attention, and then they went out for a couple weeks."

"Yeah, it might have *worked*," Zoe said glumly. "But it wasn't very smart. I made them both miserable." *And I made Caitlin and Natalia miserable, too.*

Closing her eyes, she pressed her cheek against the cool surface of the cafeteria table.

I am so bad at this.

Chapter Ten

By Friday afternoon, things between Caitlin and Natalia had, if anything, gotten worse. Neither one was speaking to the other, and Caitlin had started sitting at a different lunch table on the other side of the cafeteria, with some kids from the theater club. Natalia refused to talk to Caitlin at all, and Caitlin walked by both Natalia and Zoe in the halls without looking at them, her chin held high.

"I'm not sure why she's ignoring me now, too," Zoe said to Emma, annoyed, as they climbed onto the bus home together. Natalia was staying after school for a service club meeting, so they were able to talk openly about Caitlin and her, after keeping their mouths shut about their argument all day.

"She feels like you're taking Natalia's side," Emma

said, choosing a seat near the front of the bus, sitting down, and sliding over to make room for Zoe. "She feels like you're blaming her, when it was Natalia who pushed and pushed until Caitlin had to give her an opinion."

Zoe had noticed that Caitlin was still speaking to *Emma*. Apparently, Emma was allowed to stay neutral.

"Well, I have to be there for Natalia," Zoe said, plopping down beside Emma. "She's my *sister*. But I'm not taking anyone's side."

"I know that," Emma said sympathetically. "But Caitlin's feeling shut out."

"Only by Natalia!" Zoe said indignantly. "I'm not shutting her out—she's shutting me out!" Zoe sighed and leaned back in her seat. "I guess because she blames me for her fight with my sister. I feel awful."

The bus rattled along as they sat in gloomy silence for a few minutes. There were shouts and laughter coming from the other bus riders behind them, but Zoe was too discouraged to join in.

"You know," Emma said eventually, "maybe there's some way we can help to fix Caitlin and Natalia's friendship."

Zoe stared at her. "What are you talking about? What can *we* do?"

Emma's mouth was quirking into a smile, and her eyes were shining as if she'd had the best idea ever. "We can do *exactly* what we've been doing all month. Come up with some good advice!"

Zoe frowned, crossing her arms. "I hate to remind you, Emma, but my advice was what got us into this mess. It turns out that my advice is *bad.*"

Emma shook her head. Her eyes narrowed with determination.

At the serious look on her cousin's face now, Zoe got a sudden flashback to the beach vacation their families had taken together when they were five, and how Emma had convinced Natalia and Zoe that they *needed* to spend a big chunk of every day digging the deepest tunnel ever in the sand by the Atlantic Ocean. It didn't matter if they wanted to swim or build sand castles instead: Emma had a mission, and they were enlisted whether they liked it or not. The tide had swept away all trace of their tunnel every single night, while they'd all slept with aching muscles and gritty sand beneath their nails. Zoe really hoped that this idea would turn out better.

"You give good advice," Emma told her firmly. "It's not your fault that things went wrong this time. I bet we've helped lots of people."

Zoe sighed. "Fine. But if this goes wrong, too, I'm going to give up. I'll take a solemn vow: No more trying to tell people how to fix their problems."

"It's not going to go wrong," Emma said. "And, if it does, that won't be your fault, either."

"Okay," Zoe said. Despite her show of reluctance, she felt a little spark of excitement deep in her chest. In her mind's eye, sophisticated grown-up Zoe opened her studio door again and peeked out. Maybe her future as an artist/decorator/life-fixer wasn't impossible after all. "How do we start?"

"Let's see," Emma said. "I'll make up a letter about our problem, and we can pretend that we're on the show and that it's just something a stranger wrote, and answer it with our best advice. *Dear Zoe and Emma, One of my favorite cousins and her best friend fought and they're not even talking to each other anymore. My cousin kept asking for the friend's opinion on her work when the friend didn't want to give it. When she pushed, the friend ended up criticizing her, even though she didn't mean to hurt her feelings."*

"She's kind of blunt," Zoe added.

Emma nodded. *"Then they both said stuff that wasn't very nice, and now each of them is acting like they hate the other one. But I know they want to be friends again. They just don't know how to get over their hurt feelings."* She paused. "Is that everything?"

"I think so," Zoe said.

"So." Emma raised her eyebrows. "What's your advice? What would you tell someone else who wrote in with this problem?"

"Okay." Zoe thought. "I guess I'd say that her friends can't get to be friends again unless they talk to each other."

"Right." Emma nodded. "I'd say that the person who wrote in should try to figure out a way to get her cousin and her cousin's best friend to spend time together, preferably without fighting."

"Somewhere where they can't ignore each other," Zoe

said. "And maybe in a sort of relaxed, fun place where they can really talk. Not just at school."

"I know!" Emma said, excited. "A sleepover! They'd have lots of time to talk during a whole night spent together. And sleepovers are fun. If they're not ready to talk, they could, like, bake brownies or watch movies or something until they feel closer and are able to talk to each other seriously. We could do it at my house; we've got plenty of room on the third floor. And no little brothers."

"Neither one of them would come to a sleepover right now, though, not if they knew the other one was invited," Zoe said. "Unless . . ." The bus was getting close to her stop. She wanted to convince Emma of her idea before she had to get off. "You could invite Caitlin over to spend the night and then also invite me and Natalia, but don't let either of them know the other one is coming. That way they'd *be* there before they could start worrying about dealing with each other."

The bus rattled its way to a halt at Zoe's stop. As she grabbed her backpack and stood up, she looked at Emma. "What do you think? Should we do it?"

Emma grinned. "I think it's really good advice. I'll call Caitlin and invite her over for tomorrow night."

Zoe started walking backward down the bus aisle, giving Emma a thumbs-up. "I'll tell Natalia. Operation Secret Sleepover is officially launched!"

When Zoe told Natalia about sleeping over at Emma's on Saturday, Natalia seemed pleased, but a little subdued. Over dinner, Mateo and Tomás kept darting concerned looks at Natalia as she picked at her food.

"Come on, guys!" Zoe said enthusiastically, trying to cheer them up, and also to get them to leave Natalia alone. "Let's watch a movie!"

Tomás and Mateo followed her to the living room willingly enough, but they kept peeking back at Natalia, as if they were hoping she'd suddenly come up with a fun new game, instead of just sitting dismally at the kitchen table, picking at her nails.

Looking at their glum little faces gazing longingly back at Natalia, Zoe thought wryly: *Apparently, I'm the less fun big sister.*

Later that night, Natalia kept on being just as quiet as they both got ready for bed.

Teeth brushed and pajamas on, Zoe climbed into her bed and looked over at Natalia. Natalia was lying on her back, eyes closed, her long dark hair spreading out across the pillow. "Well, good night," Zoe said at last.

"Good night," Natalia said softly.

"Sleep tight," Zoe said.

Natalia didn't answer, and with a sigh Zoe reached over and turned off the light.

She stared up through the darkness toward the ceiling. It would be great if Emma's and her plan worked. She didn't like it when Natalia was sad.

A loud sniff came from the other bed. Zoe sat up. "Nat? Are you okay?"

Natalia sniffed again, then said in a wobbly voice, "I miss Caitlin."

"Yeah, I know you do," Zoe said sympathetically, hoping that Natalia would keep talking. It was easier to talk about feelings in the dark sometimes, when you didn't have to look the other person in the eye.

She could see the shadowy shape of her sister as she sat up on the next bed, looking lumpy because of all the blankets wrapped around her. "I know I overreacted at first," Natalia confessed in a low voice.

Zoe felt a spark of hope again. Natalia's anger toward Caitlin was clearly softening. "Well, why don't you make up with her?" Maybe the slumber party tomorrow could be a fun celebration of Natalia and Caitlin's renewed friendship, instead of an attempt to get them back together.

Natalia huffed, a sharp, exasperated exhalation. "I do miss her, a lot. But . . . it's like, Caitlin's just always so sure she's right, and she doesn't worry about anyone else's point of view. I wanted her opinion, but it wasn't fair of her to tell me I shouldn't even enter the contest because my drawing was so bad. That was just mean. And it wasn't *that* bad, right?"

"No," Zoe said honestly. "I don't think you would have won with your original drawing, but I bet most of the other entries won't be much better."

"And then her apology was basically an insult! She was like, 'Oh, I'm sorry that you're so sensitive, you big baby'!" Natalia's voice was rising; it sounded like she was getting angry again at the memory.

"That's not exactly what she said," Zoe said.

"Well, it pretty much was. That's what she meant, anyway," Natalia answered.

Zoe flopped down and rearranged the covers so they were up to her chin. Their room was chilly at night. "It's not all Caitlin's fault, either. I feel really guilty," she said. "I told her to just tell you the truth and not to worry about hurting your feelings."

"And that's another thing," Natalia said. "I can't believe she actually wrote in to your show about how bad my design was. Like, my art was an emergency she needed advice on."

"That wasn't what the letter said," Zoe protested.

"Anyway, I don't think it was your fault," Natalia told her. "I mean, the advice to tell me the truth wasn't *bad* advice. Once I realized how much work my design needed, you and I worked together and made it way better. But Caitlin made her own choice about *how* to tell me what she thought, and how to act when I got upset. And she wasn't nice about it."

"Well . . ." Zoe said slowly, "I think you said some stuff you didn't mean, too."

"Caitlin was meaner, though," Natalia said. She sounded tired and defensive. "And then I saw that she'd neatened up the work I did on our project, too. She's always got to be in charge." She lay down and rolled over with her back to Zoe. "Anyway, good night."

Zoe sighed again. *But that's how Caitlin is.* Natalia had never minded Caitlin taking charge of a project before. It was obvious how much her sister missed Caitlin— and it was obvious that she wasn't ready to forgive and forget and make friends again.

I really hope our slumber party idea works, she thought. *I want my sister back to normal.*

Chapter Eleven

"This is going to be really fun," Natalia said, hiking her overnight bag higher up onto her shoulder as she and Zoe walked up the path to Seaview House. "I'm just glad to take a break from all the drama and hang out with you and Emma."

Uh-oh. Zoe took a firmer grip on her sleeping bag, looking down at it instead of Natalia. The idea behind Operation Secret Sleepover suddenly seemed less terrific now that Natalia and Caitlin were about to see each other and find out the truth. With a shaky breath, Zoe opened the door.

"Guys! You're here!" Emma came running down the stairs, Caitlin trailing behind her.

"I didn't know you both were coming." Caitlin's voice was flat.

"I didn't know *you* were coming." Natalia dropped her bag in the entryway and looked at Emma accusingly.

"Well . . . surprise!" Zoe broke in. "Emma and I wanted to get all four of us together, to remind everyone how much fun we have as a group." She wasn't going to let the others think this was all Emma's idea. She tried to keep her voice light and cheerful, but she could feel her smile getting strained as Natalia and Caitlin both stared at her.

There was a long, tense silence.

"Maybe I should just go home," Caitlin said uneasily.

"No!" Zoe said, alarmed. She tugged on Natalia's arm, leading her farther into Seaview House. "Come on, let's all try to have a nice time. It's Emma's sleepover and she wants all of us here." Emma nodded fervently. "Give it a chance, please."

Caitlin hesitated, then looked at Natalia again, her expression closed off.

"It's fine," Natalia said stiffly. "Stay."

"Great!" Emma said immediately, clapping her hands. "Let's take our stuff up to my room and then we can make pizzas and pick a movie, okay? Dad made his special pizza dough for us to use."

"Sounds terrific!" Zoe said. She could hear that, just like Emma's, her voice sounded fake and overly enthusiastic. *But hey*, she thought, *at least we're trying*.

They dropped their stuff and started to set up.

"Wow," Natalia commented, staring up at the ceiling. "You redecorated! This looks like Zoe's influence, right?"

"Isn't it great?" Emma said enthusiastically. "It feels like spring in here now."

"It's nice," Caitlin agreed politely, not looking at Natalia.

Zoe unrolled her sleeping bag near the windows. Caitlin looked at Natalia, then looked away, while Natalia stared stonily in another direction. They both began to unroll their own bags on opposite sides of Zoe's, as far from each other as they could get while still being in Emma's room.

Emma and Zoe exchanged a glance. Were Caitlin and Natalia just going to ignore each other all night? They couldn't get to be friends again if neither of them even wanted to look at the other one. She and Emma needed to *make* Natalia and Caitlin talk.

"Okay!" she said peppily. "How about those pizzas?"

Out in the kitchen, Uncle Brian and Aunt Amy were sipping glasses of wine and laying out bowls full of toppings for the pizzas: mozzarella cheese, onions, olives, mushrooms, peppers, crumbling pieces of sausage, and even pieces of pineapple. There were four individual-sized pizza crusts laid on the table, each in front of one of the four seats.

"I prebaked the crusts a little, so you can just do your toppings and then put them in the oven for twenty minutes each," Uncle Brian said after he hugged the girls hello. "Remember to turn the oven off when you're done."

"We're going to go down and join Grandma Stephenson for dinner if you four don't need us," Aunt Amy said, adding a couple bowls of sauce to the table. Once everything was set out, she and Uncle Brian headed downstairs, leaving the four girls alone together.

"Yum, pizza time!" Zoe said quickly, sitting down and pulling Emma into the chair beside her, leaving two empty seats next to each other for the others. "Here, Emma and I will take this bowl of sauce, and you guys can take the other one." *If we just distract them from remembering they're mad at each other,* Zoe thought, *they'll fall back to acting the way they usually do together.* She spread a couple big spoonfuls of sauce across her crust and sprinkled mozzarella over it.

Caitlin glanced at Natalia warily as they both took seats in front of their pizza crusts.

"What do you think, guys?" Zoe asked, eyeing the bowls of toppings. "Would olives, onions, mushrooms, and pineapple be a weird combination?"

Emma made a face. "Ugh. I'm not sure the pineapple goes with the other things. Pineapple and onion?"

"Nonsense, it'll be terrific," Zoe said loftily. "A little dull, perhaps, I'll admit that. What if I added delicious fresh celery? There's some in the refrigerator, right, Emma?"

Emma stared at her.

"Just to add some crunch," Zoe explained.

Emma bit her lip. "How about pickles?" she offered, smirking. "We have sweet or dill. Maybe a little mustard?"

Clearly unable to resist, Natalia chimed in. "I always find that chocolate adds a certain flair to *le* pizza pie," she informed them loftily. "Just sprinkle a few chocolate chips across the top to give it zest."

Caitlin giggled. "Blueberry jam could be delightful, too," she declared, and Natalia grinned.

Zoe shot Emma a look of relief. Caitlin and Natalia were joking around! They were having fun!

The rest of the pizza making went pretty smoothly—they did *not* add mustard, pickles, celery, chocolate, or jam, but Caitlin put some pineapple slices on hers along with the sausage and seemed to enjoy it—and by the time they were eating, Zoe felt like things were already beginning to get back to normal. Caitlin and Natalia weren't talking to each other, but they were both talking to Emma and Zoe. Caitlin had smiled several times, and Natalia was grinning her big familiar grin that Zoe couldn't remember seeing at all in the last few days.

It's a good start, Zoe thought optimistically. The plan was going to work!

"Okay," Emma said, putting down the crust of her last piece. "Shall we make caramel popcorn for dessert and watch a movie?"

Once they had a big bowl of drippy, sweet popcorn, they retreated to the living room. Emma suggested a weepy teen romance that had been a big hit the previous summer and the others agreed to her choice, although Zoe would have preferred something scary or funny. But she didn't want to start trouble by arguing about the movie, not when things were going so well. They spread out comfortably over the two big couches in Emma's family's living room. Once again, Zoe moved fast and made sure to take up enough space beside Emma so that Caitlin and Natalia ended up sitting side by side.

As the girl and boy in the movie kissed on a beautiful golden beach, orchestral music swelling, Zoe let her mind wander.

Grown-up, urban, sophisticated Zoe sat at a conference

table in her office beneath one of her most beautiful paintings, smiling at the worried-looking president on the other side of the table. Next to her, Emma shook the hand of another world leader.

"Now, let's see if we can't resolve this problem, Ms. President," Zoe said, cheerfully but firmly. "There's no need to get the United Nations involved, if you and His Excellency will only talk to each other. The first step to coming to a mutually acceptable agreement is a simple conversation. I'm sure that, by starting with a low-key, relaxed chat, we will soon be able to accomplish world peace."

Zoe suddenly realized the end credits of the movie were playing.

Caitlin sniffed, wiping at her eyes. "That was so *sad!*"

"I *know!*" Emma agreed, reaching for another tissue. "I can't believe she died, when he loved her so much. And it seemed like she was getting better!"

Natalia had her hands clasped against her chest. "I wonder if anyone will ever love me enough to take me on a road trip and then stay with me through a terminal illness?"

"Let's hope we never find out," Zoe said drily.

Natalia playfully stuck out her tongue at her. "You're like the antiromantic," she said. "If you were Juliet and you met Romeo, you'd probably—"

"Live to grow up?" Zoe suggested.

Caitlin wiped away another tear. "Thanks for picking this, Emma," she said. "My mom won't let me go to this kind of movie. She thinks they're sappy and a waste of money. She says teen movies lead to brain rot."

"Maybe you should talk to her about why you want to see them," Zoe suggested. "She's a psychologist; tell her you find it healthy for your emotional development to watch sad movies."

Rolling her eyes, Caitlin laughed. "I don't think she'll go for that."

"Better not take Zoe's advice," Natalia said. She was smiling, but there was an edge in her voice. "We know how that turned out last time."

"Hey!" Zoe said, hurt that Natalia had attacked her out of nowhere.

Natalia grimaced apologetically. "Sorry, Zoe, I didn't mean your advice was bad, just that *Caitlin* shouldn't take it. But it was just a joke."

Caitlin wasn't laughing anymore. "What's that supposed to mean?" she asked coolly. "*I* shouldn't take Zoe's advice?"

"Well, she told you to be honest and instead you were really mean," Natalia said. "Obviously, you can't follow instructions very well." She twisted a strand of her hair around her finger. "I'm just kidding," she added.

No, she's not, Zoe thought. *Distracting them into talking to each other isn't really working.* She and Emma had wanted them to *talk* and have fun, not get into a fight.

"Look," Caitlin said, folding her arms over her chest. "You asked me what I thought of your design. You *kept* asking, even when I didn't want to tell you. I didn't want to lie to you. We always said we'd be honest with each other. I'm *sorry* your feelings got hurt, but let's be clear here. The problem wasn't Zoe's advice, and it wasn't that I took Zoe's advice and was honest with you. The *problem* is that *you* can't take criticism!"

Natalia bristled. "Oh, it's all me? You couldn't even let me do my part of the Egypt project without changing it!"

"I've always neatened stuff up," Caitlin said. "You

132

never minded before. You're just complaining about it now because I told you the truth when you asked me for it."

"If I'm so horrible, why are you even hanging around with me?" Natalia asked.

"Come on, you guys," Emma said, looking back and forth between them. "You're blowing everything way out of proportion."

"Emma, I'm going to call my dad," Caitlin said. "I want to go home." She was standing very stiff and straight, and her eyes looked shiny with tears. Turning on her heel, she headed for the bedroom.

Emma got up and followed her. "Caitlin, you don't have to . . ."

"Yeah, I do. I *want* to."

Zoe turned to her sister, who was staring down at the rug. "Natalia, stop her. Don't let her leave."

Natalia, without looking up, shrugged. "I'm not sure I want to stop her."

Caitlin, carrying her sleeping bag and duffel bag, came out of the bedroom and walked straight out of the apartment without looking at them, Emma following her out. Zoe listened to their footsteps getting fainter as they walked down the stairs.

"*Natalia*, stop her," she said more insistently. "She's your best friend, and this isn't worth ruining your friendship. You're overreacting."

Natalia blew out a big gusty sigh. "Stop trying to fix this, Zoe," she said. "I don't want your advice." She got up and went into Emma's bedroom, closing the door firmly behind her.

Zoe put her face in her hands. Everything had been going so well just a few minutes ago.

After a little while, Emma came back into the apartment and sat down on the couch beside her. "Caitlin's dad picked her up," she said. "She's really upset. Where's Natalia?"

Zoe jerked her head toward the bedroom. "I don't think she wants to talk to us for a while." Her hands were lying in her lap, and she stared down at them instead of looking at Emma.

Emma patted her cautiously on the shoulder. "It's not your fault, you know," she said. "I guess they just weren't ready for us to get them together."

"Yeah, I guess not." Zoe finally looked up at Emma. "Remember how I said yesterday that, if this went wrong, I was going to give up and stop trying to give people advice?"

"Oh, Zoe," Emma said. "You don't have to—"

"No, I'm serious," Zoe insisted. "Everything I've tried has just made things worse. I'm not good at giving advice. I'm sorry, but I'm not going to do the last show. I'm done."

Chapter Twelve

"You're being ridiculous; I hope you know that," Natalia told Zoe the following Wednesday. "There's no reason for you to quit the show." They were walking up the steps outside the school with Emma. Heavy, dark clouds hung overhead, gloomy and ominous, and they matched Zoe's mood. It was the last Wednesday of March, so it was supposed to be the final episode of *Zoe and Emma to the Rescue*. But, instead, it would be *Emma to the Rescue*.

"Please don't quit," Emma begged Zoe again, clasping her hands together and giving her big, sad eyes. "It's the very last show, and I'll feel awkward doing it by myself. There's nothing wrong with the advice you give."

Zoe felt a pang of guilt. It really *wasn't* fair to leave Emma to do the last show all by herself, after they'd spent the whole month doing them together. But she didn't feel like she could trust herself to give the right advice.

"I'm scared," she admitted to Emma, pausing outside the school doors. "My advice to Caitlin started the fight between Natalia and her. And my advice to Charlotte ended up making Malcolm and her both unhappy. What if I give more bad advice? I wanted to help people fix their problems, not make them worse. I trust you to give good advice a lot more than I trust myself right now."

"You gave reasonable answers to Charlotte's and Caitlin's problems," Emma said, frowning. "What happened afterward isn't all your fault."

Natalia spoke up. "Emma's right. Your advice was fine, Zoe," she said earnestly. "Yeah, Caitlin and I fought. But that was our fault, not yours. You told her to be honest. And . . ." She looked away, squinting against the wind. "It's possible that I overreacted. I just might be a *little* oversensitive about my drawing skills. And our fights after that? It was completely Caitlin's and my decision how to act."

Zoe sighed. "Maybe," she said. "But I can't help feeling like a lot of things that went wrong started with my advice. Not just with you guys, either. Think about Charlotte and Malcolm."

"Emma? Zoe?" A new voice broke into their conversation. Zoe looked up and saw a dark-haired seventh-grade girl coming up the stairs toward them. Zoe recognized Isabel Rosario, although she didn't think they'd ever actually spoken to each other before.

"Oh, hey, Isabel," she said, curious about why Isabel was suddenly coming up to her. "What's up?"

"I'm glad I saw you guys," Isabel said, smiling. "I've been wanting to talk to you."

"I'll catch you both later. It's cold out here," Natalia said to Emma and Zoe. "Bye, Isabel." She swung the school door open and disappeared inside.

"What's up?" Emma asked. "What did you want to talk to us about?"

"Well," Isabel said, and hesitated. She fiddled with her backpack strap, looking slightly embarrassed. "I was the one who wrote in to you guys about the slumber party I had? And my parents would only let me invite three people, so I had to leave one of my really good friends out?"

"Oh, yeah," Zoe said. "That was you?" Now that she

thought about it, she could picture the four girls Isabel was always hanging out with.

"Yeah." Isabel shoved her gloved hands into her coat pockets. "My friend Alice was really mad at me for leaving her out. But I took your advice. I wrote her an apology letter, and we spent Saturday down in Chestertown together, shopping and having lunch, just the two of us." She looked at Zoe. "I showed her how much she mattered to me as a friend, like you suggested, and now neither of us cares about the whole thing with the slumber party anymore."

"Really?" Zoe said, glancing at Emma. Was she listening to this?

"Anyway, I feel like you saved our friendship, and I just wanted to say thanks," Isabel said.

"Wow. Thanks, Isabel," said Zoe. She felt really touched.

"No, thank *you* guys," Isabel said, smiling.

Emma gave a little wave as Isabel headed inside. "Bye, Isabel," she said, then turned to stare meaningfully at Zoe, her eyebrows raised. "So?" she asked expectantly.

"So?" Zoe echoed.

"So, your advice really helped someone!" Emma waved her hands in the air excitedly. "Yay! Good advice!"

"*Our* advice really helped someone," Zoe reminded her.

"Yes, okay—*our* advice really made a difference for Isabel. It fixed her problem and made her life better. And it helped her friend Alice, too, because her feelings aren't hurt anymore."

"Yeah," said Zoe, pleased warmth spreading through her. Their advice really *had* helped Isabel.

"And, so, your whole point about how your advice always causes terrible trouble is just plain wrong," Emma told her. "Come on, don't make me do our very last show by myself. I'd hate it, and I don't want us to end like that."

Zoe swallowed. Emma was right. They *had* helped, and maybe most of their other advice wasn't terrible, despite what had happened to Charlotte and Caitlin. People liked their show. And Zoe realized she didn't want the show to end that way, either.

Suddenly, Zoe had an idea. "Okay, I'll do the show," she told Emma, whose face lit up with happiness and relief. "But I want to put in a new letter."

"Move your head back a little bit," Ava said, attaching a microphone to Zoe's collar as Zoe bent over the desk at the side of the room, quickly writing on a piece of paper. "Shouldn't you have finished getting your letters for the show together a while ago?"

"This one's a special last-minute addition," Zoe told her. She wrote one more sentence and then read the whole thing over. Yep, it said what she wanted to say. "Hey, Emma, will you read this one on the show?" she asked, handing the paper to her cousin.

"Quiet, everybody," Mark called, and Zoe mimed zipping her lips.

"Happy Wednesday, Waverly Oysters!" Charlotte shouted. She was grinning widely, and she had been laughing with Oliver and Shoshanna just before the show began. Even though her relationship with Malcolm hadn't worked out, Charlotte didn't seem too upset about it anymore. *I guess my advice didn't ruin her life after all,* Zoe thought. *It didn't even ruin her week.*

Charlotte and Oliver led the Pledge of Allegiance, then began to go through the morning news. As she listened, Zoe felt an unexpected wave of wistfulness. She was going to miss these Wednesday mornings. Whether the new letter she had for them to answer today did any good or not, she was glad she hadn't skipped the last show.

"We have the winner of the school T-shirt contest," Oliver announced. "And the winner is . . ." He did a drumroll on the desk, and Zoe tensed in anticipation. ". . . Elise George. Congratulations, Elise. We'll be seeing your T-shirt soon. The design will be up on the bulletin boards, and shirts will be available starting in April."

Zoe felt a little twinge of disappointment. Natalia's and her design hadn't won. She hadn't necessarily *expected* it to, but it had turned out pretty well in the end. She'd thought there'd been a chance they might win.

"Honorable mentions in the contest go to Naveen

Moore, Emily McCann, and Natalia and Zoe Martinez," Charlotte said. "Congratulations to everybody."

They liked our T-shirt idea, Zoe realized. *A honorable mention is pretty great.* Natalia was going to be so happy!

Emma squeezed her arm tight. "Congratulations," she whispered.

"And now, today is the final day of our March Wednesday show, *Zoe and Emma to the Rescue*," Oliver went on. "If you're interested in starring in our April show, please remember to submit your proposal by Monday."

Another show, Zoe thought as she and Emma switched places with Charlotte and Oliver. It was hard to believe that next week, someone else would be taking Emma's and her place behind this table on Wednesday mornings.

"Hi, everybody," Emma said. "I'm Emma."

"And I'm Zoe, and this is *Zoe and Emma to the Rescue*," Zoe chimed in.

"Today, we've got a special letter about friendship and about trying to help your friends when their friendship is falling apart," Emma said. She glanced at Zoe, and Zoe nodded encouragingly. Emma read aloud.

"*Dear Zoe and Emma, Two of my really good friends—who used to be each other's best friends—aren't speaking to each other. One of them asked the other what she thought about something important, and the friend gave her some honest criticism. So, the first friend had her feelings hurt, and she got mad. And that made the other friend mad, too. I've tried to get them to talk to each other and realize that they still care about each other and should just forgive and forget. But everything I've done has backfired, and one of them is mad at me now, too. How can I make them be friends again?*"

She put down the piece of paper. "Tough question," she said. "Zoe, what do you think?"

Zoe took a deep breath. *Treat it like it's any other question,* she told herself. *Act like it's got nothing to do with you.*

"Well, I don't think you *can* 'make them be friends again,'" she said seriously, looking into the camera. "One thing I've learned recently is that people are going to make their own choices. All you can do is support them both. Try not to take sides." She hoped that Caitlin and Natalia were both listening, especially to the next thing she was going to say. "True friends will come back together eventually. If you give them time and space to think, maybe they'll remember how much they like each other. Maybe they'll realize that their friend wouldn't hurt them on purpose. But you can't fix this for them. All you can do is be a good friend to each of them."

"I agree," Emma said, smiling warmly at Zoe. "When you care about someone, you want to fix every one of their problems, but sometimes all you can do is show you care and let them figure things out for themselves."

When the last bell rang and the day was over, Zoe, Natalia, and Emma pushed the front doors to the school open and came out through it arm in arm, laughing.

"I'm going to put our T-shirt design up on my bulletin board," Natalia said. "I don't care that we only got an honorable mention; I'm really proud of the way it turned out when we worked on it together."

"And honorable mention is pretty good," Zoe said. "A lot of people entered the contest."

"I liked yours better than the one that won, to be honest," Emma said. She let go of Zoe's arm to adjust her backpack.

"And thanks for what you said on your show," Natalia added. "I'm sorry I ruined the sleepover by starting a fight with Caitlin."

"You didn't ruin the sleepover, Natalia," Zoe said. "I shouldn't have forced it."

She and Natalia turned toward where the school buses were lined up, but Emma wasn't with them. Looking back, Zoe saw her stopped in the middle of the walkway, her face turned up toward the sky.

"What is it, Emma?" Zoe asked, concerned, turning around and heading back toward her.

"It's just such a gorgeous day," Emma said happily.

Zoe looked up at the sky, too. It was sunny and beautiful out, the sky a clear blue. A warm breeze lifted her hair, and she could smell fresh-mown grass from the lawn of one of the houses near the school.

"Let's not take the bus today," Natalia said. "It's too nice out to be cooped up in a school bus. Let's walk instead."

"All the way home?" Emma asked warily. "Because you guys live almost five miles away, and I'm another half mile after that."

"Let's walk over to the high school and ride home with Dad," Zoe suggested. The high school let out forty minutes after the middle school, so they could take their time. "Let me send him a text." Now that school was over, she could dig her cell phone out of her bag.

Text sent, she linked arms with Emma and Natalia again, and watched as people ran past them to catch their rides. As they turned and began to walk away from the school, Zoe felt Natalia stiffen. Caitlin was standing on the sidewalk in front of them.

"Hey, Caitlin," Natalia said tentatively.

"Hey," Caitlin said softly. She fiddled with the strap on her backpack.

Zoe longed to fill the silence, but she bit her tongue as the two friends stared at each other.

"Um, congratulations on your honorable mention," Caitlin said finally.

"Thanks," Natalia said. "I guess my design wasn't as bad as you thought."

Zoe grimaced. *Was Natalia ever going to get over this?*

Caitlin winced. "I really am sorry about the whole T-shirt thing. I was only telling the truth the way I saw it, but I *really* didn't mean to hurt your feelings. And I shouldn't have said any of the stuff I said later, about you acting like a baby and not being able to take criticism."

Natalia raised her eyebrows. "Are you telling me you didn't mean those things?" she asked skeptically.

"Well," Caitlin said carefully, "I did mean them when I said them, but they were only the meanest, littlest part of how I really felt. I'm not good at taking criticism, either. I guess I didn't like your criticism of my criticism."

Zoe couldn't stop a laugh, and next to her, Natalia snorted. "It does sound kind of silly when you say it like that," Natalia admitted.

Caitlin smiled hopefully.

"I guess I really just wanted you to tell me my drawing was good enough to win," Natalia said. "I shouldn't have pestered you to tell me what you really thought, if I only wanted to hear one thing."

For a long moment, Caitlin and Natalia looked each other in the eye, their faces solemn. Zoe held her breath.

Finally, Natalia smiled. "I'm sorry, too. And I'm actually glad you wrote in to Zoe and Emma's show! I never would have ended up with an honorable mention if you hadn't told me the first drawing needed more work." Linking her free arm with Caitlin's, she pulled her along with the three of them. "I missed you so much. I should have talked to you more instead of getting mad."

"Me, too," Caitlin agreed. "It's like Zoe and Emma said this morning on their show. We're *true friends*, and that means we don't want to hurt each other. Not really."

"And it means that we're bound to come back together," Natalia said. She grinned at Zoe and Emma. "Good job on the show today, guys, by the way. I'm sad I'm not going to get to watch it anymore."

"Thanks," Emma said cheerfully. "I think we have a knack for giving advice, to tell you the truth. Maybe we'll start a business at Seaview House, like your dog-walking business."

"Sure." Natalia laughed. "You could have a little table in the lobby and offer life solutions for five dollars a problem."

Zoe grinned and looked at the others. Sister, cousin, friend. All of them together, all of them laughing. She felt warm and cozy inside, like the sunshine on her skin was spreading all the way through her.

Read Natalia's story!

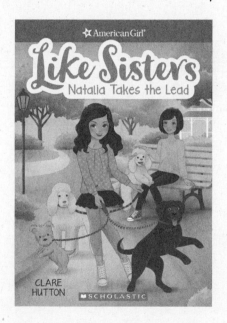

Chapter One

"Zoe! Think fast!" Natalia Martinez pitched a handful of fall leaves at her twin sister's head.

Zoe glared at her and shook her head so that the red and gold leaves fluttered to the ground. "Not funny," she said, picking a leaf out of her bangs.

Their cousin Emma, who was industriously raking on the other side of the lawn, laughed. "It's a little funny," she said.

Zoe made a face at them both, but her eyes were amused. "Messing up my beautiful hair," she complained with an exaggerated pout.

Zoe does *have nice hair*, Natalia thought.

Sometimes Natalia couldn't understand how she and Zoe could be identical twins. Right now, for instance, Zoe's preppy shirt and pants were as pressed and clean as if she'd just ironed them and put them on, even though she'd been wearing them all day. Her sleek dark bob swung neatly just below her chin, looking freshly combed.

Natalia, well . . . She glanced down at her own glittery but slightly rumpled sweater, which now had bits of leaf clinging to it, then smoothed a hand over her own long hair, which was frizzing out in all directions.

She *could* have looked as put-together as Zoe did, Natalia knew. If she wanted to get acquainted with the ironing board, and get her hair cut, and hang up her clothes as soon as they came out of the laundry, and sit and talk at recess instead of flinging herself across the playground to play tag—if she did all that, she and Zoe could look as identical as they were genetically.

But Natalia didn't care about that stuff. And Zoe did. And these differences, Natalia thought, were the real mystery.

"Twins are weird," she said out loud.

"Well, I didn't want to say anything," Emma joked, glancing up from her neat, small pile of leaves.

"I mean, look at us," Natalia said, gesturing back and forth between herself and Zoe. "For that matter, look at you. You're not a twin, but you're family. And you're the same age as us and we're in the same class at school. Why are we all so different?"

Natalia glanced around at Seaview House's wide front lawn, where they were raking. Even the lawn, Natalia thought, was like a tiny model of the differences between the three girls.

Generations of their family had lived in Seaview House, the oldest house in the small town of Waverly on the Chesapeake Bay. Just recently, Emma and her parents had moved in with Grandma Stephenson, who had gotten too old to want to live there by herself. Emma's mom was Natalia and Zoe's mom's twin sister, and they were turning the house into a bed-and-breakfast together. Emma and her parents were lucky enough to live at Seaview House. They had an apartment all to themselves on the top floor.

Natalia *loved* Seaview House, which was old in the best ways and full of cool things: a secret staircase concealed behind what looked like a regular wall, an attic crowded with stuff stored by more than a hundred years of ancestors, and a dumbwaiter, which was a tiny elevator for food. She was glad her mom and dad had bought a house just around the corner when they got married. But Seaview House had a *lot* of lawn. At their moms' request, the three girls had divided up the front lawn and had spent all Sunday morning raking it. Even divided into three, the lawn was huge, and a *lot* of work.

Emma had sectioned her part of the yard off into quarters. She worked intently on each quarter in turn, making small piles in their centers, a frown of careful concentration on her face, focused on getting up every last leaf. This was exactly what Emma was like, Natalia thought with a surge of affection: precise, and eager to do her best. Emma made lists and won swim meets and soccer games and worried about everything. She worked hard to do a good job at whatever she did.

Zoe, on the other hand . . . Natalia looked at her twin thoughtfully. What Zoe had actually gotten around to raking was almost as neat as what Emma had done. A couple mostly filled leaf bags leaned against a tree. Zoe liked to do things well, and she liked them to look *right*. But she hadn't done nearly as much as Emma, and Natalia knew it was because Zoe wasn't that interested in lawns. Right now, she wasn't raking at all, and she wasn't paying attention to what Natalia and Emma were saying, either.

Instead, she was looking at a bright red maple leaf, her head cocked thoughtfully to one side. As Natalia watched, Zoe crouched down—carefully not kneeling on the grass so that her pants stayed clean—and laid the leaf on the lawn between a smaller, almost pink one and a brilliantly golden gingko leaf.

"Oh no, we've lost her to the colors again," Natalia said to Emma. Zoe didn't even look up.

Zoe loved her family and her small group of close friends. She was snarky and funny and smart. But what she was most interested in was painting and drawing and making things. She could get swept up in examining a contrast of color or working on a sketch, and Natalia could see everything else melt away for her sister, leaving only the colors or the drawing.

Natalia herself didn't especially want to be able to

draw, but she couldn't help envying Zoe a little. Zoe knew what she was good at, knew what she was passionate about. Natalia did lots of stuff—theater and service club and volunteer work—but she didn't have one special interest or talent like Zoe did.

So, if Emma was careful and conscientious and Zoe was wrapped up in her art, what was she like? Natalia wondered. She looked at *her* part of the lawn. There was one big pile in the middle of her section of the lawn, bigger than any one of Emma's or Zoe's piles, but there were still tons of leaves threaded through the grass as well.

Natalia made a face. "Ugh, *why* do I have so many leaves left? I've been raking like crazy!" She had been putting all her energy into it, dragging huge rakefuls of leaves across the lawn. Why wasn't she as close to done as they were?

Zoe, distracted from her contemplation of colors, snorted.

"What?" Natalia asked, putting her hands on her hips.

"Well," Emma told her, exchanging a glance with

Zoe, "it's true that you've been working really hard. When you're working. But you keep getting—"

"Hello, girls!" Mrs. Lau from down the block was waving at them from the sidewalk, where she was pushing her baby in a stroller. Emma and Zoe both waved. Natalia hurried over.

"Hey, Mrs. Lau!" she said. "Were you guys down by the water?" She puffed her cheeks out at baby Charlie, making him giggle. "You like the beach, don't you, Charlie?" Charlie made babbling noises and reached up toward her, and Natalia took his plump little baby hands and smooched them.

She and Mrs. Lau chatted for a couple minutes. When Mrs. Lau and Charlie moved on, Natalia spotted old Mr. Ainsley, another neighbor, washing his car, and ran across the street for a minute to say hello.

When she came back, Emma raised her eyebrows pointedly.

"What?" Natalia asked.

"You were wondering why you haven't gotten a ton done?" Emma reminded her. "It's because Mr. Ainsley was probably the eighth person you've stopped to talk to since we started."

"I *like* to talk to people," Natalia said defensively. She reached down and picked up her rake. "Besides, I couldn't be rude and ignore them."

"You want to be friends with everybody," Zoe diagnosed. She reached down and pulled a lemon-colored leaf out of her pile and held it up, peering at it against the sun.

"Well . . . yeah," Natalia said, puzzled. Who *wouldn't* want to be friends with everybody? "Of course I do."

Emma leaned back against a tree and smiled at her. "And that's why we love you, Natalia," she said.

Seaview House's front door burst open as Natalia and Zoe's little brothers, six-year-old Tomás and five-year-old Mateo, ran outside, across the front porch, and down the steps to the lawn. Their elderly family dog, Riley, followed more slowly, puffing a little, and lay down by the front walk, his tail wagging.

Mateo and Tomás didn't stop. "Can't catch me!" Mateo screeched tauntingly, and sped across the lawn, running straight through Natalia's big pile and scattering two of Emma's smaller ones.

"Stop!" Zoe yelled, running to intercept the little boys as they headed for her part of the lawn. She was too late. Tomás tackled Mateo straight into the side of one of the bags full of leaves she'd raked and it toppled, spilling them between the trees. "No!" Zoe said, grabbing another bag to steady it before it fell, too. "Cut it out, you guys!"

"Keep them over there!" Emma called, hurriedly re-raking her own pile. "I'll come help you in a minute."

Natalia stuck two fingers in her mouth and whistled, a loud, shrill note. Mateo and Tomás untangled from each other and looked up at her, blinking.

"Come on!" she said cheerfully. "We'll play a game." The boys scrambled up and came over. She looked around her section of the lawn, a plan beginning to take shape. "Here," she said, handing her rake to Mateo. "We'll make a maze. And when we're done, Zoe and Emma will have to find their way through it."

Tomás nodded enthusiastically and started pushing

the leaves into walls, but Mateo leaned on the rake and frowned.

"We don't have enough leaves," he complained. "Emma and Zoe will be able to see over the walls."

"We could get leaves out of the bags," Tomás suggested.

"No, don't do that," Natalia said, seeing Emma's horrified face. "It would be cool to make really huge walls, but I'm not sure how we'd keep them up." She remembered a maze she'd seen once at a park. "What if instead of the kind with high walls, we just used low walls to mark out our maze?"

She crouched and picked up a stick to sketch a square in a nearby patch of dirt. "Pretend this is the maze. We could put the entrance here and the exit here." She drew little lines to show where she meant. "We can make it as complicated or as simple as we want—we just need to make sure there's only one way to get to the exit."

"We could make it look like a path by letting them get this far and then putting a wall," Tomás said, taking the stick and making scratches of his own. "They'll be so mad!" He giggled.

Once they'd marked out all the twists and turns, building the maze wasn't too hard. They all ran back and forth for a while, looking at their drawing before Natalia realized it would be easier to stand by the plan and direct Mateo and Tomás.

"Okay, Mateo," she said, squinting at the plan. "Put a long line of leaves up to where Tomás made the turn."

"What are you, the General of Leaves?" Zoe called teasingly from across the lawn.

"I'm the Commander of Autumn!" Natalia called back. "Obey me!" Emma and Zoe both rolled their eyes, but the boys, who loved playing army, saluted.

"Hut, hut, hut, double time," Natalia ordered. "Get those leaf walls built up, soldiers!"

There were long lines of red, yellow, and brown leaves crisscrossing Natalia's whole section of the lawn. "Almost ready," Tomás said, excited.

Zoe shook her head as she stuffed her last armload of leaves into a trash bag. "You know you're going to end up having to rake that whole side of the lawn again."

Natalia sighed. It was true. Still, at least the leaves

were all neatly laid out. Probably she and the boys could just scoop them up.

"Don't worry, we'll help you," Emma said supportively.

Zoe grinned. "I suppose. But only if the maze is fun."

The maze *was* fun.

"This is actually impossible, isn't it?" Emma asked, a line of concentration appearing between her eyebrows.

"You're never going to get it!" Mateo teased, jumping up and down, and Zoe and Emma both groaned.

Tomás, looking sympathetic, whispered loudly, "Emma! Turn here!"

Natalia flopped down cross-legged on the lawn to watch Zoe and Emma puzzle their way through. Riley, wagging his tail, walked over stiff-leggedly and collapsed next to her, putting his head in Natalia's lap.

"Hey there, good boy," Natalia said, playing with Riley's long, silky ears. "Whatcha doing? You want to play?" Riley woofed softly and closed his eyes.

"You all look busy." Her mother's amused voice came from above her, and Natalia twisted around to look up at her.

"Hey!" Natalia said. "I didn't hear you come out." Then she remembered what she was supposed to be doing and grimaced. "Sorry, we *were* raking, I swear."

"I know," her mom said, smiling. "But come on inside, because Aunt Amy and I have news for you." She raised her voice. "Emma! Zoe! You, too."

Emma was just triumphantly stepping out of the maze. "What?" she said. "We're going to clean it up! It's not Natalia's fault!"

"Well, it actually is," Zoe muttered, still stuck halfway through the maze. At Emma's look, she sighed and added, "But we are going to help clean up."

"You're not in trouble," Natalia's mom said. "Just come inside. We have something exciting to tell you."

In the elegant front room of Seaview House, Emma's mom, Aunt Amy, was waiting. Natalia and Zoe's mom sat down next to her on the long velvet settee and waved the girls into cushy armchairs.

As Natalia looked at her mom and aunt, she was reminded again of how different she and Zoe were, because their mom and Aunt Amy, who were twins, too, were just as unlike each other. Aunt Amy, who had been a lawyer in Seattle before coming back to Waverly, looked very businesslike. She had short, neat hair and wore blazers and nice pants and shoes with a low heel on them. Natalia's own mom was more a classic-mom type: shoulder-length hair, sweaters, and sneakers. But they shared the dream of turning Seaview House into a bed-and-breakfast, and they worked together really well.

"So what's up?" Zoe asked curiously.

Natalia's mom and Aunt Amy looked at each other. "Well . . ." Aunt Amy said, drawing out the anticipation, ". . . we have our first guests!"

"What?" Natalia said. "That's amazing!" Zoe and Emma cheered. Her mom and Aunt Amy had been working on fixing Seaview House up for months and, except for a reception for friends and family, they hadn't opened for business yet. Apparently, getting ready for guests took a *long* time.

"We have two couples coming for three full weeks. They're friends and they're traveling together," Natalia's mom said. "They sounded lovely on the phone."

"We could work to make their stay better. I can help Dad in the kitchen," Emma offered. "I like cooking."

"Do you want me and Zoe to wait tables?" Natalia asked. "That could be fun."

Zoe frowned, twisting a strand of hair around her finger. "Do I have to? I'd rather make beds or something like that. I don't want to have to talk to strangers first thing in the morning. Ugh."

Their mom laughed. "Don't worry, Zoe, I think we can handle four guests. We can come back to the idea when the bed-and-breakfast starts getting busier. But if we ever do need you girls to help out, it'll be your choice. And I imagine you'd get paid."

"Well, congratulations," Emma said. "The guests are going to have a great time."

"I hope so." Aunt Amy sighed. "Each couple is bringing a dog with them. They asked if I could recommend a dog-walking service or doggy day care around here, but I couldn't. They decided to come anyway, but it means they'll have to schedule their days around walking the dogs."

Zoe and Natalia's mom shook her head. "I really wish

we could have found another option for them. Those dogs are going to get restless."

A brilliant idea hit Natalia, and she bounced in her seat. "What if *we* walk the dogs? I love dogs!"

Her mom and Aunt Amy exchanged a look. "Are you sure?" Aunt Amy asked. "You'll be responsible for taking them out twice every day. If you're going to do it, you'll have to make a commitment and stick to it."

"Of course we'll stick to it," Natalia said.

"I want to help," Emma said hesitantly. "But I've got soccer practice twice a week and games as well. And swim team practice, too."

"And I'm going to do theater club with Natalia this year," Zoe said, not making eye contact with anyone.

"You *are*?" Natalia asked, distracted. Zoe had never wanted to sign up for theater club before. "Are you going to paint sets?"

Zoe's cheeks were turning pink. "I might try out for Dorothy," she mumbled. "I really like *The Wizard of Oz.*"

Of course. Natalia knew that was her sister's favorite musical. "I think that's great," she said decidedly. "You've got a way better singing voice than I do."

Zoe peeked at her from the corner of her eye. "Do I?"

"You really do," Natalia assured her.

"It sounds like you girls are pretty busy," Natalia's mom said, biting her lip. "It's a good idea, though. Maybe there's someone at your school who would like—"

"No!" Natalia said. "We want to do it. Come on, you guys. There are three of us, and only two dogs, for just a few weeks. It'll be easy."

"Well . . ." said Emma.

"I guess . . ." said Zoe.

"Awesome," Natalia said confidently. Between the three of them, they'd have plenty of time. "We'll do it," she said to her mom and Aunt Amy. "Trust me, it'll be a piece of cake."

A group of girls so close, they're just

Like Sisters

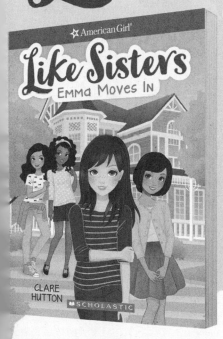

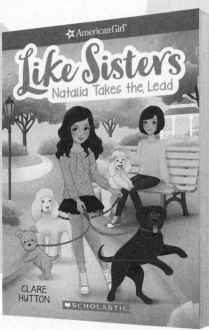

Emma loves visiting her twin cousins, Natalia and Zoe, so she's thrilled when her family moves to their town after living 3,000 miles away. Emma knows her life is about to change in a big way. And it will be more wonderful and challenging than any of the girls expect!

There's going to be a wedding at the inn—with dog ring bearers! Natalia loves dogs and offers to watch and walk them. But has Natalia bitten off more than she can chew? When one of the dogs goes missing, Natalia enlists Emma, Caitlin, and Zoe to help. If they can't find the dog, the wedding will be wrecked!